SHERLOCK HOLMES IN PURSUIT

by

Matthew J Elliott

Published in the UK by MX Publishing
335 Princess Park Manor, Royal Drive,
London, N11 3GX
www.mxpublishing.com
Cover design by www.staunch.com

The stories *The Adventure of the Patient Adversary*, *The Adventure of the Mocking Huntsman*, *The Adventure of the Honourable Cracksman* and *The Adventure of the Extraordinary Lodger* originally appeared in *SHERLOCK* Magazine.

The Adventure of the Forgetful Assassin was first published in the collection *The Game's Afoot*.

The Adventure of the Hanging Tyrant was first published in the collection *Curious Incidents 2*.

CONTENTS

The Adventure of the Patient Adversary   4

The Adventure of the Mocking Huntsman   28

The Adventure of the Forgetful Assassin   52

The Adventure of the Honourable Cracksman   76

The Adventure of the Hanging Tyrant   98

The Adventure of the Extraordinary Lodger   157

THE ADVENTURE OF THE PATIENT ADVERSARY

It is now many years since I published my account of Sherlock Holmes' dramatic return to London which I entitled *The Empty House*, and the details are now well known to the public. But even after the arrest of Colonel Sebastian Moran, the second most dangerous man in London, I found it hard to believe the whole incredible affair had not been some weird dream. I was grateful for the newspaper reports of the incident for they served to remind me that I had not imagined the entire thing, and that my good friend was not merely alive but thriving. For some time after Holmes had reclaimed our old bachelor rooms on Baker Street, I retained my medical practice in Kensington, although with the possibility of the renewal of our adventures constantly on my mind, my professional duties seemed increasingly less absorbing. Matters came to a head in the April of 1894 with the arrival of a letter from Angus Molesworth, a fellow student during my days at the University of Edinburgh. Molesworth, I recalled, had never been what I would term an intimate acquaintance, for he had inherited his father's haughty manner and military bearing. It was indeed peculiar that it should be I, not he, who ended up in uniform and under fire on a foreign shore. I had not heard from him in well over a decade, and the content of his letter took me by surprise completely.

Aberfeldy, Winchester

My Dear Watson:

Please excuse both my boldness in writing to you after all these years and the brevity of my communication. I prefer not to dictate my letters, but anything over a page exhausts me these days.

I was astonished to read that your friend, Mr Sherlock Holmes, is not dead as had been reported and furthermore that he has resumed his former profession as a consulting detective. Do you think that you could bring Mr. Holmes down to see me? I should like to have his opinion of a quite urgent case. You are my first port of call, Watson, as I am certain that he must have many demands upon his time but I hope that our previous association might hasten an introduction. Please make it plain to your friend that time is of the essence, this is a case of murder. I shall explain more when I see you both.

Your old fellow-student
Angus Molesworth

There was something that touched me as I read this letter, to note how a man so full of pride and his own self-importance had now been reduced to pleading with one of his former friends – and not a close friend, at that - for assistance. From the reference to exhaustion and the weakness of the handwriting, I deduced that Molesworth must be seriously ill. I determined that not a moment should be lost in laying the matter before my old friend and former colleague, and so within the hour I found myself back once again in our old rooms in Baker Street. 'Watson, you could not have come at a better moment,' said Sherlock Holmes as he put a light to his cigarette. 'Oh, you have a case, then?' I asked.
'On the contrary, no case of any sort has come my way since my return to England. The typical Londoner is a cautious and cynical fellow who no doubt suspects that the reports of my resurrection are a devious ploy calculated to boost the circulation of *The Strand* magazine. As a result, I am sorry to say, I am at something of a loose end. In times gone by, I might have craved the relief afforded me by an injection of a cocaine solution.'

I restrained my desire to question the use of the word *might*. 'But,' I reminded him, 'you disposed of your hypodermic syringe when your feud with Professor Moriarty began in earnest.'

He smiled wistfully at my mention of his old arch-enemy. 'In those days, Watson, I had no want of mental stimulation. The Professor was a worthy adversary, and we shall not see his like again.'

'Thank heavens,' I breathed.

'Help yourself to a cigarette, and tell me all about the acquaintance who wishes to avail himself of my services.'

'This is too much!' I cried. 'Have you abandoned conventional detective work in favour of mind-reading?'

'My eyes are the only tools I require to delve into the thoughts of another. I see, I observe. In this instance, I observe your ill-concealed disappointment at the possibility that I might already be engaged upon an investigation. How unlike the Watson of yesteryear. Secondly, I observe the letter thrust hastily into your pocket. I observe further that it is in a man's hand. I do not believe that I am hazarding too much to say that the letter is from an acquaintance, asking that you enlist my aid in unravelling some mystery. You still have the envelope, I trust? Excellent.'

'It seems quite simple when you explain it.'

'Every problem seems quite simple once it has been explained,' he replied, a trifle nettled. He studied the letter in silence for some time. 'The handwriting is interesting,' he said, at last. 'Your correspondent is in poor health.'

'So it would appear,' I agreed, 'and yet I remember Angus Molesworth as a hale and hearty fellow in his youth.'

'*Tempus edax rerum*, Watson. The writer is clearly unwell, and yet he insists upon writing his own letters. Does that indicate strength of character or distrust of those around him? And yet, there is one in the house whom he trusts somewhat more than the rest.'

6

'How can you be certain of that?'

'The envelope, Watson - it is in a different hand. Evidently, the writer put his faith in another individual to address and perhaps even post his *crie de coeur.*'

I was gladdened that the letter had clearly piqued Holmes' insatiable curiosity, for I was anxious to be off. So great was my haste, in fact, that I quite forgot to call in at the house of a patient and provide him with an eyedropper to ease his chronic allergic conjunctivitis.

Holmes' trusty Bradshaw advised us that the next train to Winchester was at half-past ten, allowing barely sufficient time in which to telegraph news of our intentions to Molesworth before heading for the station. It was some two hours later that we found ourselves in a carriage driving out from the centre of the old English capital. Aberfeldy proved to be a large detached house standing in extensive grounds. The maid answered the door to us, and we were led into a spacious study, where we were greeted by a round-faced young man with straw-coloured hair, who introduced himself as Molesworth's secretary, Mathew Cranmer. Evidently, Molesworth's private practice was more fruitful than I had imagined. I was somewhat surprised not to be met by his employer, however.

'For the past month, Dr Molesworth has been confined to bed,' Cranmer explained.

'What ails him?' I enquired.

The secretary frowned. 'Dr Synott is expected shortly. I really think it would be best if you waited for his arrival. I'm sure he will be happy to answer any questions regarding Dr Molesworth's condition.'

'Is Molesworth's doctorate of a non-medical nature, then?' Holmes asked.

'The doctor is in no fit state to diagnose himself,' Cranmer snapped. 'I doubt if he is even well enough to speak to

you, Mr Holmes, but he has been awaiting your arrival
ever since he wrote to Dr Watson. If you will follow me,
gentlemen, Dr Molesworth is in his room.'
I wondered about Cranmer's apparent desire to be as
unhelpful as possible. Did he indeed wish to be
obstructive, or was he merely protecting his employer? He
certainly had no difficulty in meeting my gaze, but that in
itself was hardly conclusive proof of virtue.

The bed was in the centre of the room, and in it, propped
up with pillows, was the owner of Aberfeldy. When one
believes oneself untouched by the passage of the years, it
is always a shock to discover how much an old friend has
aged. The gaunt, wasted face staring at me from the bed
sent a chill to my heart, for when I had seen it last, it had
been full, healthy and pink.
Angus Molesworth lay listlessly as we entered the room,
but the sight of me brought a gleam of recognition to his
eyes.
'Watson, my dear chap,' he gasped. 'Please allow me to
keep what remains of my dignity, and refrain from telling
me how well I appear. I am perfectly well aware that I
look abominable.'
'The years have taken their toll on us all, Molesworth,' I
replied. 'I am now, as you see, substantially larger about
the middle. Only last month, I bumped into Casper
Holland – he is now quite bald.'
'Bald? Good gracious me.'
For Molesworth's own sake, I had no wish to prolong such
idle banter. 'Angus,' I said, using his Christian name for
the very first time, 'this is Mr Sherlock Holmes.'
'Of course,' Molesworth croaked, stretching out a bony
hand in greeting. 'Who else could it be? I hope, Mr
Holmes, that Watson does not exaggerate your gifts in his
stories. He always was such a one for tall tales.'
'The good doctor has an appalling habit of romanticising

8

my little exercises in logic, but the essential facts are invariably accurate.'

Molesworth gave a weak smile. 'Won't you please both be seated?' He turned his head to face Cranmer, the secretary. 'Mathew, perhaps you would care to go downstairs and keep a lookout for Dr Synott.'

The young man said that he would prefer to remain, but Molesworth made it plain that he wished to speak to us privately.

'He's a good boy,' he told us after Cranmer had reluctantly departed, 'and fearfully protective of me.'

'It was he who addressed the envelope?' Holmes suggested.

'Yes, I would have preferred to address it myself, but I was all done in by the time I finished the letter. Robert Cranmer was my best friend from childhood. When he died, I tried my best to be like a second father to young Mathew, who was his only son. I have no family of my own, so perhaps I have acted out of purely selfish reasons.'

'Dr Molesworth, you say in your letter that you wish me to investigate a case of murder. Who has been murdered?'

'I have, Mr Holmes.'

My companion's expressive face showed a sympathy which was not, I am afraid, entirely unmixed with excitement at the anticipation of a fresh and challenging investigation.

'I am dying, as you see,' Molesworth went on. I began to protest, but he raised a hand to silence me. 'Please, Watson, I do not have the strength to argue. There is one who wishes me dead, and matters have been arranged so as to ensure that I meet my fate in the most agonising manner possible. Mr Holmes, there is a letter on the dresser. Please read it.'

Holmes took the thin sheet of paper and examined it. Seated beside him, I was able to read it without too much difficulty, despite the fact that it was written in a hand more erratic than Molesworth's own.

Molesworth (it read)

Retribution is upon you at last. By 7 October, you will be dead.

Unsurprisingly, there was no signature.
'The writing is disguised,' Holmes observed.
'Written with the left hand, no doubt,' I suggested.
'Something far simpler and effective. The paper has been held against the trunk of a tree. The variations in the bark disguise the handwriting quite successfully. If any doubt still persists' - he reversed the paper and indicated several patches of a light green substance – 'tree fungus. We can therefore say with confidence that the letter was written on the north side of the tree, not that it does us any good. Regrettably, I am unable to determine the particular type of tree. My knowledge of practical gardening is quite limited, I regret. Do you have the envelope?'
'Mathew threw it away, unfortunately. At the time, it seemed unimportant. The handwriting was the same, of that I am certain. And there was no postmark.'
'October the 7th - does the date hold any special significance for you?' Holmes asked.
'Yes, it is the date of the attack on the Forbidden City in China by English and French forces in 1860. That devil will not let me forget.'
'What devil?' I asked.
'Professor Chen Ta-kai, the noted chemist. You recognise the name, Mr Holmes?'
'I do,' my friend replied. 'I have travelled a good deal during the past three years and I have heard his name mentioned in connection with many mysterious occurrences around the world. I believe that he takes no

active part in crime, but wherever there is a relative whose continued existence bars the way to a massive inheritance, Professor Chen Ta-kai is on hand to provide the means to dispose of that inconvenient individual. His extensive knowledge of poisons makes him the ideal criminal advisor. I had a premonition that our paths might some day cross. I should be most interested, Dr Molesworth, to learn how you came into his power.'

'It was five years ago, and I was attending a medical conference in Cologne. Chen had been invited to talk on his extensive knowledge of some quite obscure treatments, many of them completely unknown in the West. He had written a piece for *The Lancet*, I recall - totally unintelligible to me.

'He was quite a sight at such a staid affair – a brightly coloured robe that reached the floor and covered his feet entirely, a moustache so long the ends touched his chest. His face was large and round, I recall. But those eyes… I will never forget those eyes. They were not blue or brown; they seemed to me to be totally black. I have never before seen such a thing, and it was quite unnerving enough in and of itself.

'His grasp of the language was superb, far superior to mine. My attention lapsed after about half an hour. I then realised to my surprise that those unsettling black eyes of his were fixed upon me. He continued to stare at me for the remainder of his lecture. It was a most unnerving experience. After the talk was over, he sought me out.

' "Forgive me," he said, "my knowledge of English not so good as my German. You are, perhaps, the son of Colonel George Molesworth?"

' "You have met my father?" I asked, somewhat surprised.

' "Once only. You resemble him to a great degree. I would wish very much to speak to him. Your father, he still lives?"

' "No," I replied, "he died some years ago, of pancreatic

11

cancer."

'At last he lowered his gaze. "Then he is beyond retribution."

' "I beg your pardon?"

' "He perhaps told you how he murdered my own father, who was employed at the Yuanmingyuan, the Garden of Perfect Splendour?"

'This allegation took me by surprise. It angered me, of course, but I had no desire to create a scene. I knew that the old man had played a part in the invasion of the Forbidden City all those years ago, but little more than that. "My father never talked much of his time in Pekin," I told him, "so I am unable to respond to your claims, except to say that many tragedies occur in warfare. For that, you have my sympathies."

' "I watched my father die," he said, without a trace of emotion. I looked into his eyes, expecting to see cold cruel menace, but all I saw were the twin reflections of my rather startled expression. "He was shot down while trying to protect the Black Jade of the Imperial Concubine, Yehonala. Colonel Molesworth fired that shot and stole the Black Jade."

' "If there was ever such a thing as Black Jade in my old man's life, I can assure you I never saw any of it, so if you're hoping to get it back I'm afraid you're clean out of luck," I replied, coldly. In truth, I recalled that he had meetings with several private art collectors at one time, but I was still young then and had taken no interest in his affairs.

' "The Jade was never mine to reclaim," said he. "What I desire, you cannot provide. Instead, I can only promise you that you will die on the same day my father was murdered by the man whose blood surges through your veins. Good-day to you, Dr Molesworth. Please enjoy the rest of your stay in Cologne."

'With that, he simply turned his back on me and strode

12

from the room. At first I was dumbstruck by the fellow's audacity, but when I came to myself, I attempted to catch up with him and have it out there and then. To my astonishment, he was nowhere to be seen. He had somehow vanished as though he had never been there at all, and I have not seen him again from that day to this.'

'And yet you accuse him of poisoning you?' Holmes asked.

'I do not accuse, Mr Holmes, I know it. Of course, at the time I thought it some sort of weak threat. As the years went by, I began to think of it as an example of the peculiar humour of the Chinese. But last month, the letter arrived, and almost immediately, I fell ill. Since then, I have not had the strength to leave this room.'

'And the cause?'

'Poison, naturally. But how he is feeding it to me, I have no idea. One thing I do know, Mr Holmes, and that is that he will keep me alive but in this feeble state for the next six months as punishment for the death of his father. On the seventh of October, he will have made his point and I shall breath my last.'

'Did you relate your conversation with Chen to anyone else?'

'Mathew, of course. He was not with me at the time, but afterwards…' Molesworth was tiring rapidly and his voice began to fade.

Holmes realised this, and his questions took on a note of urgency. 'Who else apart from Mr Cranmer?'

'Dr Synott, I think… Can't remember. Help me, Mr Holmes. Help me before it is too-' The interview had clearly put him under severe strain, and he lapsed into unconsciousness before he could finish.

We rose to leave, and were met at the door by Cranmer who informed us that Dr Synott awaited us in the study.

The doctor proved to be a smart, keen-faced fellow in his

early thirties. He greeted us with surprising enthusiasm.
'I have longed to meet you both, gentlemen,' he said,
shaking us both vigorously by the hand, 'but after reading
of your death, Mr Holmes, in one of Dr Watson's
accounts, I never thought this day would arrive. I only
hope, sirs, that you are able to succeed where medicine has
failed. To speak frankly, Mr Holmes, you are Dr
Molesworth's only hope.'

'Your patient is of the opinion that he is being poisoned,'
Holmes said.

'I have to say that I agree, but I can find no positive proof
to confirm that. I have performed every test I test I can
think of and consulted every specialist I know, but
whatever substance has been used cannot be ascertained.'

'What are the symptoms?' I asked.

'Extreme fatigue, muscular pain, loss of appetite. He
grows no worse, but his condition never improves. He has
been confined to his sickbed for a month. My first thought
was that the poison might have been added to his food.'

'What steps did you take to pursue this notion?'

'None, there was no need. Dr Molesworth had Mr
Cranmer dismiss his cook immediately and take on a
replacement the same day.'

'That seems somewhat drastic,' I observed.

'It certainly did not make him popular with the original
cook, but it at least eliminated the possibility that the
poison was being added to his meals.'

'Did the rest of the staff receive the same harsh treatment?'
Holmes enquired.

'The servants have been in his employ for several years.
Their loyalty is beyond question.'

'And what of Mr Cranmer's loyalties?'

Dr Synott appeared ill at ease with this line of questioning.
'As far as Dr Molesworth is concerned, he is above
suspicion,'

'Is that your opinion also?'

'I have no reason to believe otherwise. Perhaps you will think it peculiar, Mr Holmes, but I even considered writing to this Professor Chen for his opinion. I mean, on the off-chance that Dr Molesworth is mistaken and this Chinese fellow is entirely guiltless. If he is as clever as he is made out to be, then it would be a crime not to make use of that knowledge.'

'A response from Pekin may come too late to save your patient,' I suggested.

'Not from China, Doctor, from Camberwell. That is where he is living at present, I understand. I have this from a colleague.'

'Did this colleague provide you with an address in Camberwell?' Holmes asked.

Synott shook his head. 'I'm afraid you'll have to find that out for yourself, Mr Holmes.'

After Synott left to continue his rounds, promising to return in the morning to look in on his patient, we went for a turn around the garden, and took stock of all that we had learned thus far.

'I believe Molesworth told us that he had no family,' mused Holmes. 'Were he to die, would Mathew Cranmer be the sole inheritor, I wonder?'

'But surely Angus does not have enough money to prompt a man to murder, Holmes?' I protested.

'I have seen instances of men struck down for a few coins.'

'It seems to me that the best course of action would be to locate this Chen Ta-kai.'

'That is precisely what I intend to do, Watson. In the meantime, you must remain here.'

'I, remain?' I protested.

'Molesworth's condition has remained constant for the past month. There has been no improvement, nor has there been any sign of deterioration. I think we may take it as a working hypothesis that he is being poisoned regularly, each time with the same dosage. If you can identify the means by which he is given the poison, we may be able to put and end to it. You must be my eyes while I am away, Watson.'

I must confess that his show of confidence gave me keen pleasure, for I had often been piqued by his indifference to the attempts which I had made to assist him in his investigations.

Thus encouraged, I dashed off a note to my neighbour asking him to look after my practice for a day upon our return to the house. I had performed the same favour for him on several occasions and he was always ready to work off the debt.

'That reminds me,' I said, handing the note to Holmes, 'I meant to deliver a prescription to a patient, but in all the excitement I forgot about it. If you end up spending the night in London, would you be so good as to deliver it?'

'Well, the resumption of my work as a consulting detective has been less fruitful than I hoped. Perhaps I should consider seeking fresh employment as a postman.'

'I wish you luck in Camberwell,' I told him, 'although I cannot help but wonder why this Chinese professor should wait five years before carrying out his threat.'

'Poison is the weapon of the patient man, Watson. You recall that the threatening letter stresses that Molesworth faces retribution "at last". I do not relish the prospect of finding myself retained by a corpse. Let us hope that my conversation with Chen Ta-kai sheds some light upon the matter before Dr Molesworth is beyond our assistance.'

After Holmes' departure, I searched the still sleeping Molesworth's room, hoping to find some indication of how the poison was being delivered. There was nothing suspicious about the ventilator, and I rang the bell-pull to ascertain whether or not it served some other function –

16

Cranmer and the maid arrived in something of a panic. After assuring them both that there was no emergency, I resumed my search, to no positive result. By the end of my investigation, I slumped back in my chair, defeated.

At about midnight, Molesworth's strength rallied, and we talked for several hours of our days as medical students. The conversation was a rather dispiriting one, for we shared few happy memories of time spent in one another's company.

'If I could live my life over again, Watson,' he said, before slipping into another deep slumber, 'I would do everything differently. Do you understand? Everything.'

At seven in the morning, the maid appeared, bearing a jug of water and a bowl for his morning ablutions. It was difficult for me to watch an old associate, a man of my own age, struggle with the straightforward act of washing himself, but Molesworth would not hear of my offer of assistance, and I understood that to accept my help would be to admit defeat and acknowledge the fact that he truly was dying.

An hour later, Mathew Cranmer arrived with a breakfast tray. I took care to sample each item so as to pronounce them safe for consumption, but Molesworth had little appetite and could not be persuaded to take more than a couple of mouthfuls of scrambled eggs.

I read to the patient for several hours. How much of it he took in, I could not say. I admit to having no recollection now of either the book or its author.

Quarter of an hour before lunchtime, Dr Synott called as promised and was shown up to the bedchamber. I studied Synott's ministrations intently, hoping that in my friend's absence my eyes would prove equal to the task. But though I sought not only to see but to observe, there appeared to be nothing untoward in the doctor's treatment of his failing patient. I doubt that I could have done any more for Molesworth. Eventually he departed, having performed no miracles but – so far as I cold make out – having done nothing to worsen his patient's condition, either.

Molesworth would have none of his lunch, a small sandwich, and I took no pleasure in the little that I ate. Time passed as painfully slowly as it had at the base hospital in Peshawar. Then, I had been the patient. Now, I was an onlooker. But where my wounds had eventually healed to a satisfactory degree, Angus Molesworth's continued survival lay not in the hands of any doctor but with a consulting detective. But I had known Holmes to discover truth where others saw only chaos. If any man alive could solve the mystery of Molesworth's terrible predicament, that man was Sherlock Holmes.

As I mused on this, I must have closed my eyes, for the next thing I knew, I was being shaken awake. Instinctively, my hand reached for my old service revolver before I realised who had roused me.

'Holmes! When did you arrive?'

'Quite some time ago. Our client has quite an extensive library of medical texts, and I have been immersing myself in it to no avail. Even Chen's original article in *The Lancet* provides no clues.'

'You located Chen?'

'In a house in Camberwell, fronted by a small garden decorated exclusively with rhododendrons. He was much as Molesworth described him – polite yet impudent, and clad in a vibrant robe that put my mouse-coloured dressing gown to shame - but he omitted one significant detail about the man.'

'That being?'

'His total malevolence, doctor. The man emits evil like an odour, it surrounds him. Too long in his company and one might find it suffocating.'

'This is not the sort of talk I am used to hearing from you, Holmes,' I commented.

'It is certainly less than scientific, but the fact that evil cannot be measured does not mean that it does not exist.

'I was met at the door by a Lascar servant, monstrously tall and sporting a hideous scar, running from his forehead to below his left eye. I looked in upon Lestrade after my visit, and he informs me that the description matches one Ram Singh, a former member of the Spencer John gang, and a useful fellow in a knife fight. The Professor knows some nice people! They are no doubt strange additions to the otherwise mundane lives of their neighbours. I saw Chen in a sitting room that looked as out of place in Camberwell as a fine gem in a setting of brass. From floor to ceiling, he had done his utmost to conceal all that was suggestive of the European. Brightly-coloured cushions and a rich Persian rug obscured the carpet, silk screens adorned the walls, and where once there had been a traditional light fixture, there now hung a paper lantern. My nasal passages were at once invaded by a sharp, brackish odour, which I identified as emanating from a small cup on a low table by my host's chair.

' "I prefer to sit on cushions when taking tea," he explained, pleasantly, "but I am aware that you might find such a practice undignified. Might I offer you a cup?"

' "No, thank-you," I replied, "I did not acquire a taste for green tea during my time in Tibet. No doubt you are aware that consuming it in excessive quantities causes delusions?"

' "Naturally. But, forgive me, you did not come to my lowly house in order to impart a warning on the dangers of tea drinking."

' "I wish to speak to you about Angus Molesworth," said I. "He is near to death."

' "So I have heard," he answered, displaying not a hint of passion.

' "Is that so? From whom have you heard?"

' "The British medical community gossip like a group of

old women. I doubt that there is a doctor in the south of England who does not know of his malady."

' "He accuses you of poisoning him."

' "Indeed? Most gratifying. And quite understandable. I did, after all, threaten his life."

' "Then you admit your guilt?"

' "I admit nothing." The Oriental features flickered, and I imagined for a moment that I could discern a flicker of amusement in his eyes, but I could not be certain. They are as our client recalled, as black as ink and impossible to read. I wonder, in fact, whether he might not be a follower of Franz Mesmer. That would certainly explain his hold over Molesworth in Cologne.

' "If he is dying," Chen continued, "then he is dying. If you can uncover proof of my complicity, then I am guilty. You are the detective. I have read many accounts of your triumphs. Your mind functions in a manner that is almost Chinese."

' "I relish the compliment.'

' "Forgive this unworthy individual's show of pride, but after reading of your miraculous return to life, I had hoped that Dr Molesworth would request your assistance."

' "And why is that, pray?" I asked.

' "You are famed throughout this land for your observational skills. The eyes are important to you."

' "I have had some success in placing guilty men on the gallows, certainly."

' "You expect to see me stand on the gallows, then? Do you subscribe to the belief, made popular by your nation's cheap fiction, that the Chinese are a devious race, consisting solely of thieves, assassins and opium addicts?"

' "By no means, Professor. Had we the time, I would relate to you the details of one of my earlier investigations in which I was able to overturn just such a presumption. But I fear that every hour I spend away from Dr Molesworth, his life remains at risk."

' "While I remain here. Unless, of course, you believe that a man such as I could roam the streets of an English village unobserved? I have only to step into my garden to excite conversation."

' "Your objection is a reasonable one," I informed him, "but the person responsible for the poisoning of my client clearly possesses a brilliant mind."

Chen gave a slight bow. ' "That is a considerable compliment – to the poisoner, whoever he may be. Perhaps my own knowledge might prove of some assistance in this matter. You are aware, perhaps, that a powerful poison may be obtained by the process of boiling the leaves of the rhododendron?"

' "The poison in this case thus far defies identification. It appears to be unknown to science."

' "To *Western* science. There are many types of poison known in China that have never been seen in your country. Poisons undetectable by any Western medicine. Perhaps one of these substances has been used to bring about his much-deserved death."

' "Have a care, Professor," I cautioned him. "To some ears, your remark might sound very much like a confession."

' "I confess nothing. If, as I have said, you are able to discover proof of my guilt, that is something else again. You are aware, Mr Holmes, that no two finger-marks are alike?"

' "Of course - Monsieur Bertillon's famous discovery."

' "For many centuries, the Chinese have known of the individuality of the finger-mark. If you are successful in locating the bottle of poison that is being used to slay your client, and if you can find upon that bottle the finger-marks of my wretched self, you will be in position to have me arrested. But not, I suggest, before." Rising from his chair, he picked up the delicate cup and placed it on my palm. It still contained traces of dark leaves floating at the bottom. "I have handled this item many times," he said. "You will find what you require there. A goodwill gift from a humble admirer."

'I left him then, confident that he would say nothing incriminating. If Chen imagined that I would leave the cup behind, he was disappointed. I spent the evening at Baker Street going over my records in the hopes of finding a similar crime. It has long been one of my axioms that there is nothing new under the sun, but this case appears to be something entirely original.'

'Do you believe that the poison is derived from the rhododendron as Chen indicated?' I asked.

'Not for a moment. The poison extracted from the leaves of the rhododendron is acidic in nature. He was taunting me, Watson, almost gleefully. No, as he indicated, Chen is obviously using something he brought back from China.'

'You are quite certain of his guilt, then?'

'All my instincts cry out that he is guilty, but the fact do not support that belief. The answer is right before my eyes, of that I am certain, and yet I am unable to see it.'

Several minutes passed in silence, and I knew better than to interrupt the flow of his thoughts at such a time.

When I felt the moment to be appropriate, I said: 'Did you, by any chance, perform that errand I asked of you?'

'Forgive me, Watson, but I can spare no thought for any other matter. I hope your patient will not suffer unduly if he is forced to wait until tomorrow.'

'By no means as much as Molesworth,' I replied with solemnity.

I described to him the day's events, who had come and gone, and all that I had observed. Or, rather, failed to observe.

'You have done splendidly, Watson. I really doubt that I could have done any better. I'm sure that you must crave a proper night's sleep, and your patients must have need of you. Why do you not take the next train back to London, while I keep watch here? I shall inform you if anything of significance occurs.'

Four days passed, during which I heard nothing from either Sherlock Holmes or the occupants of Aberfeldy. So busy was I with my professional duties that I had neither the time nor the energy to venture out to the nearest telegraph office and send an enquiry to my friend. On the fifth day, I received a short, brusque note from Angus Molesworth, thanking me for persuading Holmes to take an interest in his case but giving no indication of his condition or how matters had turned out in my absence. I was coming to the end of the letter when Sherlock Holmes arrived, the mischievous twinkle in his eyes indicating that he had much to report.

'I observe that the quality of Dr Molesworth's handwriting has improved,' he said, seating himself in a rocking chair. 'At least, as much as any medical man's.'

'Holmes,' I pleaded, 'do not keep me in suspense any longer! What has been going on?'

'It has been a fascinating experience. Perhaps if you were to accompany me to Camberwell for the final act of this little drama, it might be of considerable interest to you. That is, if you are interested in these little problems of mine. Lestrade will meet us there.'

Needing no further persuading, I snatched up my hat and stick, and was on the doorstep before Holmes had risen from his chair.

The scarred Lascar servant who opened the door to us started upon seeing Lestrade; clearly he recognised the police inspector. After he led us into the sitting room, I fancied I heard the front door open and close again as he fled the premises. Certainly, he was no longer present at the conclusion of our interview with his employer. Chen did not rise to greet us, nor did he register any surprise when Holmes introduced one of his companions as a Scotland Yard inspector.

'I have come to inform you, Professor,' said Holmes, 'that your assistance in the Molesworth matter will not now be required. Inspector Lestrade has already made an arrest.' The professor raised a quizzical eyebrow. 'Indeed?' he said in an amused tone. 'I am most gratified to hear of it. Tell me please, who it is that this worthy gentleman has detained.'

'Dr Molesworth's maid,' Lestrade explained. 'I recognised her at once as one Catherine Ellis of Hounsditch. We've been looking for her since she murdered her husband four years ago.'

'There has not been time to ask her how your paths crossed, Professor. I should be fascinated to hear the story from your own lips.'

'I do not understand the meaning of your words, Mr Holmes.'

'You understand all too well, Professor. Catherine Ellis has been in your employ for some considerable time.'

'I can only answer that I do not know this person.' I was struck with the same revulsion for this villain as Holmes had experienced upon his previous visit.

'She claims otherwise,' my companion countered. 'She says that you persuaded her to take the position as Molesworth's maid some three years ago.'

'Lies.'

'She says that one month ago, you provided her with a bottle of poison and instructed her to place a small amount in his food. Not enough to kill him, but sufficient to incapacitate him.'

'Lies.'

'Thereafter, she was to add a few drops to the water he used to wash each day. The poison was not ingested as all supposed, but absorbed through the conjunctival membrane. One of Dr Watson's patients is suffers from

24

conjunctivitis. He recommended that an eyedropper be used to ease the problem. When I recalled this, my own problem began to ease. I was certain that upon our first meeting you were taunting me by dangling the answer in front of my face. Then I recalled your words: "The eyes are important to you".'

'My faulty English, I think.'

'Forgive me, I think not. I imagine you had it finely calculated, Professor, so that Molesworth would remain in a weakened state until, at last, he would die on the very date of your father's death, thanks to a much larger dose of the poison. In that way, at the moment of his own death, Molesworth would know for certain that you were his executioner, but he would know also that there would never be any proof of the fact. After I requested that Mrs Ellis drink a toast to her employer from the water she brought to his room for his morning ablutions, she was most forthcoming in return for the opportunity to decline my invitation. She gave you up in a moment, Professor. She told me that you paid her fifty sovereigns a year to play the role of Molesworth's maid and gain his trust until such time as you chose to put your iniquitous plan into action.'

Chen displayed a weary grin. 'More lies.'

'I have seen the money.'

'Nevertheless, I did not give it to her.'

'I have also seen the substance used to poison my client. Once I had the bottle in my hands, I wasted no time in delivering it to the famed chemist Sir Carmichael Pertwee, who eventually identified the liquid as the fabled *Zhen* Bird Solution, which is obtained by pouring rice wine over the feathers of the Crested Serpent Eagle. An obscure potion, to be sure, but by no means incurable. You will be distressed to learn that Dr Angus Molesworth is now quite comfortable.'

The Chinaman bore his defeat with such a fixed

expression of serenity that I might have believed him totally innocent of any wrongdoing.

'You have found the poison bottle?' he asked.

'I have.'

'And have you discovered my finger-marks on that same bottle?'

'I have not.'

Chen appeared to consider this point. 'Then, forgive me, but you have no proof to put before honourable British jury. Only the word of a murderess, a devious and untrustworthy person.'

'You go too fast, Professor. I may have been unsuccessful in discovering your finger-marks on the poison bottle, but I did, however, discover them on the gold sovereigns in the possession of your confederate.'

Chen Ta-kai's jaw dropped. He wanted to respond but shock prevented his vocal chords from functioning.

'Do you believe, Professor, that an honourable British jury might find another explanation for the presence of your finger-marks on those coins?'

At last he spoke, and his reply was no more than a whisper. 'I believe… that they might have some difficulty in doing so.'

But the end of the affair proved not to be as neat as Sherlock Holmes had anticipated. For though Chen was as docile as a lamb when Lestrade led him out to the waiting brougham, by the time the vehicle arrived at Scotland Yard it was found to contain only a pair of unlocked handcuffs and an unconscious police inspector. Lestrade later recollected that Chen had produced from the gaping sleeves of his robe a small glass phial. After that, he remembered nothing until he was roused from his drug-induced slumber an hour later.

Holmes was of the opinion that the felon had returned to China, but nevertheless Angus Molesworth went into seclusion following word of his adversary's escape, and I have heard nothing from him in the intervening years. Regrettably, the same proved not to be true of Chen Ta-kai, who re-emerged to trouble us again during the affair I set down as *The Adventure of the Honourable Cracksman.*

'The Professor should be commended for his extraordinary patience,' Holmes commented upon hearing of Lestrade's mishap. 'It has been my experience that crimes of vengeance always follow quickly upon the heels of the cause. If Dr Molesworth had fallen ill immediately after Catherine Ellis entered his service, she would have been suspected immediately. As it was, Chen allowed several years to pass before initiating his scheme.'

'A scheme that would have been successful had it not been for your extraordinary powers of observation and deduction, Holmes,' I added.

'No, Watson, I cannot take credit for this little victory. I have no doubt that at the back of your mind you had some notion of the way in which the poison was being administered. Clearly, that is what reminded you of your patient's eyedropper. It was only by your mention of it that I was able to ascertain the connections in this peculiar chain of circumstances.'

I smiled to myself. For some weeks, I had been pondering what to do about my medical practice, but at last I had made my decision. It seems that I am as susceptible to flattery as any professional beauty. 'Thank-you, Holmes,' I said. 'I don't believe I could have done it entirely without your help.'

THE ADVENTURE OF THE MOCKING HUNTSMAN

With the arrival of the new century, I saw less and less of my friend Sherlock Holmes. My second marriage had drifted us away from one another and we corresponded little, the telegram remaining Holmes' preferred method of communication. The installation of a telephone in our old Baker Street rooms tested, rather than strengthened, the bonds of our friendship. Many was the night when, after an exhausting day at my practice, I would be awakened by the ringing of that instrument, and answer it only to hear Holmes say: 'Watson, come here, I want you', before terminating the call abruptly. From such instances I gathered that the detective was - despite his advancing years - still alternating between ambition and rheumatism, and wished me to join him so that he might have the entire collection of appurtenances without which he would feel incomplete.

A spell of unseasonably pleasant weather seemed somehow connected to an outbreak of good health among my patients and, finding that I had, for once, time on my hands, I determined that I should call upon Holmes.

'You come at a propitious moment, Watson – I am expecting a client within the hour. I fear the luncheon you have asked Mrs Hudson to prepare will have to wait.'

'My hearing is growing less acute as I get older, Holmes, but it seems that yours only becomes stronger. You heard my conversation with Mrs Hudson in the kitchen?'

'I heard nothing.'

'Then how on earth…?'

'The present Mrs Watson obviously keeps you on a tight reign where your dietary habits are concerned. Your clothes tell me that you finances give no cause for anxiety at present, so this is not a question of penny-pinching. Clearly, your wife is interested in reducing your girth. You have lost seven pounds since I saw you last.'

'Seven and a half.'

'Just a trifle less, I fancy. You have time on your hands, but you have chosen to spend it not at home but at Baker Street, where Mrs Hudson can be relied upon to ease your hunger pangs with her over-generous servings.'

'Well, I actually came to see *you*, Holmes,' I objected, before adding, weakly, 'but I generally have a small something about now.'

Holmes burst out into a roar of laughter. 'Good old Watson! How I have missed you these past few months. Could both your wife and your practice spare you for a day or two? According to his letter, my client hails from Mithering in Berkshire.'

'Well, I had promised to take Kate to the new play at the Trafalgar this Friday.'

'Times change, my dear Watson, and you run the risk of becoming a fixed point. The Trafalgar is now The Duke of York's.'

'It will always be the Trafalgar to me, Holmes. But if this business does not last more than a day or so, I do not see that my patients will come to any great harm...'

Mr Aldous Cadwallader represented everything I have come to despise in the provincial lawyer. His gold-rimmed spectacles were perfectly round, his suit neatly pressed, his grey beard recently trimmed. I took pains to avoid paying excessive attention to his nervous tic – the only chink in his armour of smugness. He spoke to Sherlock Holmes in the excessively polite tones of one who has no regard for his fellow man whatsoever.

'What exactly is the matter you wish me to investigate, Mr Cadwallader?' Holmes asked.

'No matter, Mr Holmes,' the lawyer responded, with an arrogant shake of the head.

'No matter?'

'It is my client, Mr Ambrose Scullion, who desires to engage your services. I wish to state at the outset that he takes this course of action in direct defiance of my counsel. I am, nonetheless, duty-bound to put the matter before you, but I understand fully if you do not wish to accept Mr Scullion's case.'

'On the contrary,' Holmes replied, with gleeful malice, 'I think it extremely likely that I shall accept. Please state the nature of your client's problem.'

The lawyer grumbled and his neck gave an involuntary spasm.

'Mr Scullion wishes you to investigate the murder of his grandson, Gideon.'

'And you do not?'

'To pursue the matter would be a waste of both time and money. The killer, who wishes to be known as the Huntsman, has completed his stated task, and has doubtless fled the area.'

'Stated task? He sent a letter, then?'

'Hmph! I should call that an elementary observation, wouldn't you? This was received the day after Gideon's murder. It was found on the doorstep by the valet, Seabury.' He removed a crumpled piece of paper from his pocket. Holmes took the note and examined it under his convex lens, before emitting a snort of disgust.

'The letter has clearly been through many hands,' he said, bitterly. 'Any significant indications have doubtless been obliterated. Beyond the obvious fact that it is written in a disguised hand by a man, I can deduce nothing.'

Cadwallader permitted himself a self-satisfied chuckle. 'I did warn Mr Scullion that he expected too much from you, Mr Holmes. The London papers are clearly too easily impressed by your pronouncements.'

'Kindly read it aloud, Watson,' said Holmes, ignoring our guest's intolerable manners.

I took the note and read: ' "My Deer Mr Scullion,

' "The time has come fore you to suffer as I hav sufered under yore hand. Eckspect no leniency. Remember Norborough.

' "The Huntsman".'

'He struggles with the spelling of the word "dear",' the detective observed, 'but has no difficulty with the word "leniency". Also, the writer is undecided on whether to mis-spell "suffer". An educated man posing as an uneducated one.'

'Our own Sergeant Merriman deduced that some days ago, Mr Holmes. I must confess, I was hoping for something a little better.'

'From your lack of enthusiasm, Mr Cadwallader, I assumed that you hoped for nothing at all. Who is Norborough?'

Cadwallader emitted a false guffaw and wiped away a non-existent tear of mirth. 'Oh, that *is* rich! Not who, but where, Mr Holmes. Do I take it that you have never heard of the Norborough mining disaster of '76?'

'I have some vague recollection of it. What is Mr Scullion's connection with this incident?'

'Why, he owned the mine that collapsed, of course! Some fifty men died in the cave-in, a further twenty in the rescue attempt, my client's own son among them. Following that… regrettable incident, Mr Scullion lost all enthusiasm for commerce. He sold his mining concerns both here and in Australia, and relocated to Mithering, the behaviour of a vocal and ungrateful minority in Norborough having made life intolerable there. He has been content to live off his profits and those of his forebears ever since. Gideon he took with him, and raised him as a son.'

'What became of the boy's mother?' I asked.

'She took her own life, not six months after her husband's death. A woman of rather weak character, I always thought.'

Holmes rapped his pipe upon the arm of his chair. 'Please

state the details of Gideon Scullion's murder.'

'Last Wednesday, he went for a stroll on his grandfather's estate, Orlando Park. He did not return, and Seabury subsequently discovered him dead with a bullet in his back.'

'That is a most concise account,' Holmes observed, dryly. 'Can you add nothing more?'

'I am not the detective, Mr Holmes. If there is more to be found out, it is up to you to find it.'

'And you believe that Gideon Scullion was killed in revenge for this incident?' I asked.

'I repeat, sir, I am not the detective. I do not propose to do your thinking for you. However, it seems to me perfectly obvious that some deranged individual has taken the life of Ambrose Scullion's grandson as punishment for that dreadful occurrence, despite the fact that he was found to be innocent of any negligence. The train for Norborough leaves in one hour and a quarter. I suggest that we leave at once. You will be able to commence your investigations before the day's end and bring them to a conclusion all the sooner. I am sure that you will understand if I accompany you. I wish to ensure that my client's money is spent wisely.'

'Surely it would be sensible to commence investigations in Mithering,' I suggested. 'There is nothing in the letter to suggest that Ambrose Scullion is not in danger also.'

Cadwallader's twitches became more pronounced. 'It would be a waste of a bullet, doctor. Ambrose Scullion is a desperately ill man. Gideon was the last living member of his family. He now lives only to see the murderer punished. Mr Holmes, the Norborough train...' He produced a gold hunter and waved it impatiently.

Holmes grimaced. 'Mr Cadwallader, I regret that I cannot leave immediately. There are still one or two matters in connection with the shooting at Royston Manor I have yet to clear up. However, I suggest that you go to Norborough this instant and secure accommodation for us. I am certain that I shall be able to join you by early evening.'

Cadwallader grumbled to himself again, but said that if it must be so then it must, and he would leave at once.

Holmes watched from the window as the solicitor hailed a cab before crying: 'Watson! Scribble down a note for your wife, saying that you have thrown in your lot with me. We leave for Mithering this instant!'

As we settled into our compartment on the train, I put it to Holmes that Cadwallader would doubtless be annoyed upon discovering that we would not be joining him in Norborough.

'There is something in Mr Cadwallader's nature that causes me to take the path opposite to the one he insists upon. Of course, he could simply be what he appears – an officious oaf, jealous of anyone who might rob him of a portion the small degree of influence he possesses. But there is another reason that this case piques my interest.'

'That being?'

'You will recall, Watson, the similar matter in which we were involved in Penzance in '95, or the numerous attempts upon the life of Major Desmond. In both instances our investigations uncovered a good deal more than seemed apparent at first. Perhaps my decision to accept this case is based entirely upon either sentimentality or a desire to be obstinate, in which case I fear that my emotions have finally overtaken my reasoning and my retirement from the world of detection cannot be far away.'

Before leaving Baker Street, I had snatched up both a sandwich prepared by Mrs Hudson – which I now consumed - and a collection of recent newspapers, which I scoured in hopes of finding a more detailed account of the murder of Gideon Scullion. My search was rewarded with the discovery of a report in the *Standard* which I read aloud:

' "Mr Scullion had recently returned from Norborough, the town of his birth, where he had been visiting his friends from childhood, the Troughtons. Upon his return to his grandfather's home, Orlando Park at Mithering, he expressed a desire to stretch his legs and announced that he would take his grandfather's Russian wolfhound, Finbarr, for some exercise on the estate, which is of a not inconsiderable size. Some three hours later, the young man had not returned and concern for his well-being was expressed. This concern deepened when the wolfhound was heard howling at the back door, having returned without his master's grandson. A search of the estate was organised with justifiable rapidity, for the body of Gideon Scullion, killed by a single bullet wound to the back, was discovered less than an hour later by the valet.' "

As I refolded the paper, Holmes wondered aloud, 'If, as Mr Cadwallader asserts, this crime has its roots in Norborough, why did this Huntsman not seize his chance when Gideon Scullion was on his territory?'

'Perhaps he did not know of it,' I suggested.

'You believe that the arrival of a member of the town's most notorious family caused no comment whatsoever? It will not do, Watson. You know as well as I the value of local gossip.'

'Well, perhaps the Huntsman had already left for Mithering.'

'In which case, our most sensible course of action would be to discover if he remains in the region and where he is presently staying.'

It seemed that we had had left the fine weather behind us in London, for the climate in Mithering had a bleak, Autumnal quality, well-matched to the disposition of the locals. Even the cab driver who transported us to the local inn, *The Prancing Pony*, did little to disguise his mistrust of the two strangers who occupied his carriage. He refused to be drawn by Holmes' casual questions regarding recent arrivals in the area.

My companion was as easily influenced by his environment as all great artists, and felt the atmosphere keenly. 'I do not think I have seen such an inhospitable town since my student days, Watson,' he observed, as we drew to a halt at the door of the tavern. From its name, I had fully expected *The Prancing Pony*, at which we were able to secure rooms without difficulty, to be a lively and charming establishment. However, an air of oppressive gloom hung over the place, which the proprietors, Mr and Mrs Smallwood, did nothing to allay. Husband and wife - both tall and wiry with long, gaunt features - seemed excessively dour for the owners of a rural hostelry.

'We stop serving at sundown, gentlemen,' the landlady advised us morosely. 'Folk won't drink any later with that – that madman on the loose.'

Given the assurance of Cadwallader that the shooting of Gideon Scullion had been a personal matter, directed at the victim's grandfather, I was taken somewhat aback by the panic felt by Mithering's inhabitants.

When our hosts were out of earshot, Holmes remarked, slyly, 'It has been my experience that pets often take on the characteristics of their owners. I am beginning to form the opinion that, given sufficient time, the same process occurs to married couples. There may even be a monograph in it. I say, landlord!'

'Yes, Mr Holmes?' Smallwood responded, dragging his feet as he made for our table.

'Are there any other inns at Mithering?'

'We are the only one, sir,' he replied, cautiously. 'You might always try the nearby towns. Are the rooms, then, not to your liking?'

'They are entirely satisfactory,' Holmes was quick to reply. 'I wish merely to obtain some local information.'

'I am afraid I cannot assist you there, Mr Holmes. As you will hear from our customers, my wife and I are new to the area, and we will not be staying.'

'Oh?'

'You have doubtless heard the story of the Huntsman?'

'He was responsible for the killing of old Ambrose Scullion's grandson, was he not?' I asked, as casually as possible.

Smallwood glowered at me, and for a brief moment, I thought he might even attempt to strike me.

'It does not surprise me,' he said, 'that the newspapers choose only to relate the death of a wealthy young man, but the Huntsman has taken another life two days ago. My own brother, James, who came down to visit us from Leigh.'

'Kent?'

'Lancashire, sir. We are recently settled in the area, and Jimmy decided to look in upon us, and see how we were getting on. Early next morning, he took a stroll in the woods from which he did not return. I called upon our local policeman, Bob Merriman. We found Jimmy's body in the early hours of the next day… He was the only family member I got, sirs, just like young Scullion was to old Mr Scullion, but I don't suppose anybody cares about that.'

'I offer my sincere condolences for your loss, Mr Smallwood. Forgive me, but- your brother so recently murdered, and yet you continue to manage this establishment?'

Smallwood bowed his head. His features were lost in shadow. 'My wife and I are new to these parts, doctor, and know no-one who might run this place while we mourn. Mr and Mrs Breelander, from whom we purchased *The Prancing Pony*, have retired to the Cotswolds. And we must stay open, at all costs. Business has dropped off dramatically since these killings began.'

36

I looked around the room, and discovered that we were not quite alone, as I had supposed. An elderly man supped slowly from a pint of ale in a dusty corner.

I was overcome by a sense of profound embarrassment. Having originally categorised our hosts as surly and mistrustful of strangers, I now understood that they had good cause to be despondent.

When Smallwood returned to his post behind the bar, I wondered aloud why the lawyer Cadwallader had not seen fit to apprise us of this development.

'I think it best,' said Holmes, 'that we see our client before his representative realises that he has been duped and returns from Norborough.'

Despite the presence until recently of a young master at Orlando Park, the gardens had been allowed to get into a terrible state. We stepped over a felled and long-dead beech tree on our way up the drive. It would surely not have been difficult for the Huntsman to select an effective hiding place hereabouts.

Seabury the valet – still much unnerved by his recent discovery of Gideon's body - escorted us into the presence of Ambrose Scullion. It was still light, and not especially chilly outside, but we discovered the elderly mining king sat close to a blazing fire, a large wolfhound which I presumed to be the devoted Finbarr curled up at his feet. The extreme gauntness of our client's features and the greyness of his loose skin told me of the monumental hurt he had suffered with the loss of his late brother's son. He appeared not to notice when Seabury announced us, and we stood awkwardly for a moment before he spoke at last.

'I have attended Sunday mass for more years than I am able to remember, but I am not a religious man. I cannot subscribe to the belief that we are all – how does Gertrude put it? – "Passing through nature to eternity". I fear death, gentlemen, as much as I did as a child. But now I long for it. I am tired with a life that has robbed me of every member of my family and left me behind, as though forgotten by oblivion.'

'Your entire family, Mr Scullion?' I asked, somewhat sceptically.

'Gideon's father, my own son, died in the Norborough disaster in '76. Gideon was still a child then. He lost his mother – a lovely, fragile creature – a few short months later. My own brother, Evelyn, suffered a fatal heart attack not long after he and his wife had relocated to America. Evelyn always had something of an eccentric frame of mind, and fancied that he future of the civilised world would depend some day upon the United States. I understand he fathered twins while out there… Evelyn, named for himself, and John for our own father. But I was never destined to see them, for they and their mother were killed in a train crash in Alabama a few years after my brother's death. I do not know whom I pity the more: that poor woman and her boys for dying so young, or myself, left to bear the grief. I am not a religious man, as I say, but I do not allow a day to go by without a prayer for those boys. It is painful, even at my great age, to acknowledge that too often the answer to our prayers must be a refusal…'

Ambrose Scullion continued for some time in this vein, describing the fates of various branches of his family, before it became clear to us both that we were no longer being addressed and that our host had quite forgotten we were even present.

It is always distressing to observe a once strong and imposing personality reduced to a confused wreck by physical and emotional impediments. In my capacity as physician, I have seen more examples than I should wish.

In my years of association with Sherlock Holmes, I have seen many country police stations, so it came as no great surprise to me that Mithering's was little more than a cottage, transformed into an official building by the inclusion of a cell in the back room. The local sergeant, however, was not at all as I had expected. Young and lean, Bob Merriman looked every inch the typical Scotland Yard official. He was well-groomed in all aspects of his appearance, from his wardrobe to his neatly-trimmed ginger moustache. I found his steely gaze somewhat disconcerting.

'Mr Holmes, Dr Watson,' he greeted us as he lowered himself into a rickety chair behind the well-worn desk. 'I was advised by Mr Cadwallader that Ambrose Scullion has requested your involvement in this business. I am surprised not to see Aldous with you.'

'I would not dream of stealing that gentleman away from his normal duties which are no doubt extremely pressing,' Holmes replied, flatly.

'No doubt,' Merriman repeated slowly. 'I will do you the courtesy of being frank, Mr Holmes. I am an extremely ambitious man. I aim to be an Inspector before the year is out. The capture of the Huntsman will be a feather in my cap, and I mean for him to be caught before a Scotland Yarder turns up to claim all the credit, which will surely be in a day or so. Your assistance, gentlemen, is welcome so long as I think it in my interest to accept it. Should I feel, however, that you are becoming a hindrance…' He left the sentence incomplete.

In former times, Holmes might have grown enraged with such impertinence. I have seen him belittle much older and higher-ranking officers. Now, he simply gave a tight-lipped smile. 'You are refreshingly blunt, Mr Merriman. I hope that Dr Watson and I do not fall short of your expectations. Now, as to the matter of the Huntsman?'

'People 'round here are frightened, Mr Holmes. A personal matter this may be – a "vendetta", I believe they call it abroad – but Tom Smallwood's brother is an innocent victim of this madman and unless some action is taken one of the townsfolk may be next.'

'What action do you propose?' I asked.

'I propose to hunt the Huntsman. Every able-bodied man in the district will be gathering in the woods at six this evening, and under my guidance we will run this fellow to ground. You gentlemen are quite welcome to join us. I fancy that the Huntsman probably uses a Lee Enfield. The sort with the long magazine, not the new type.'

'What makes you so certain, Sergeant?' Holmes asked.

Merriman shifted uncomfortably. 'I use one myself, Mr Holmes. Hunting is a hobby with me. My father, may god give his soul rest, taught me when I was a lad.'

I indicated a map of the district, which hung on the wall behind Merriman. 'Where do you intend to begin your search, sergeant? Surely the fellow could be hiding anywhere.'

'Not just anywhere, doctor. He is in the woods, for that is where we found his den, not far from James Smallwood's corpse. A crude affair, disguised with a sheet of bed-linen covered in leaves and soil. Seemingly, Smallwood came across the Huntsman in this lair, and paid the price for it.'

'It strikes me that the Hunstman is making his situation unnecessarily complicated. He might just as easily have adopted a disguise, secured accommodation nearby, and vanished when his task was complete.'

'Is that Mr Holmes' idea of things?' Merriman asked with a sly grin.

I flushed. 'I have made a few embellishments of my own.'

'Watson and I are of the same mind on this matter. Did you discover no other clue?'

'There were burn marks on Smallwood's wrist and face, as might have been made by a lit cigar. It would appear that the Huntsman tortured him.'

'To what end, I wonder,' Holmes mused.

'And end is not always required, Holmes,' I pointed out. I

had seen on more than one occasion during my brief military service the depths to which men were prepared to sink if circumstances were sufficiently pressing.

Merriman removed a sheet of paper from his desk drawer. 'In the pocket of Smallwood's coat, I found this,' he said. Holmes took the leaf and examined it. 'I can say with confidence that it and the previous letter are the work of the same hand.'

I took a copy of the message for my records. It read:

"Mr Skullion,

"You are not the man that will be blamed for nothing. Another innosent death is on yore head. The police will never catch me but they are well come to try.

"The Huntsman"

'Once again, our correspondent overdoes his part,' Holmes observed. 'The name Scullion is spelled correctly in the first letter. What are your thoughts, Watson?'

'The grammar is atrocious,' I commented, 'but the meaning is clear. He is mocking us.'

'I fancy he will have less to laugh about when he is locked in my cell tonight,' Merriman remarked with, I thought, unwarranted confidence. We left him to his thoughts of glory and promotion.

'Watson, does it strike you as peculiar,' Holmes asked as we walked the empty streets, 'that the warning letter should be delivered *after* the murder of Gideon Scullion? The purpose of such a missive is normally to instil fear in the recipient. Here, the act has already been performed.'

'Unless the elder Scullion is the Huntsman's second target.'

'It is certainly a possibility. Why do you suppose that – if the killer acts out of revenge for the Norborough tragedy, as Cadwallader believes – he has waited over a quarter of a century to strike?'

'I considered that,' I responded, 'and it is my belief that the Huntsman is not a survivor of the disaster, but the son

41

of one of the miners killed in the collapse. With adulthood, he can now exact retribution upon the man he considers responsible for his father's death.'

'Sound reasoning, Watson.'

I started at the realization of the consequences. 'Then Cadwallader may be correct and the Huntsman is back in Norborough!'

'*Rem acu tetigisti*, Watson. In which case, he is effectively waiting to be arrested. A day or so cannot make any difference. But if he remains in Mithering, there may still be considerable danger.'

At *The Prancing Pony*, we partook of a dispiriting meal of some undercooked and indeterminate species of fish served by a taciturn Mrs Smallwood, before setting out on foot for Mithering Woods.

We were, it appeared, the last to arrive, for an enormous crowd of what must surely have been all the town's young menfolk were assembled, some bearing torches, others firearms. I was not surprised to observe the landlord of *The Prancing Pony,* a pistol in his fist, no doubt hoping to avenge his brother's death.

From the map on Merriman's wall, the woods did not appear vast, but the reality was somewhat different. 'One might expect to see Red Riding Hood running from tree to tree,' I commented.

'You know my feelings on *that* story, Watson.'

Sergeant Merriman, his rifle at the ready, stamped over to greet us. 'Glad you could join us, gentlemen. This strikes me as the best place to start our search, for the body of Smallwood's brother was found here.'

'And the Huntsman's lair?' Holmes enquired.

'A little over in that direction. But I assure you there is nothing to discover, I have searched quite thoroughly.' He turned to face the masses, and began the task of organising the hunt.

Merriman's assurances notwithstanding, we headed off in the direction he had indicated, and Holmes spent some twenty minutes poring over the killer's makeshift den, while I paced up and down, attempting to keep warm and berating myself for not keeping one of Mrs Hudson's sandwiches for such a moment as this.

'You present an easy target, Watson,' said Holmes, rising to his feet. 'The Huntsman could hear your rumbling stomach yards away. Was the fish not to your liking?'

'I shall be generous, and attribute the poor quality of Mrs Smallwood's cooking to her grief for the loss of her brother-in-law. Did you discover anything of significance?'

'There is something amiss here, Watson. No ashes from a fire, no remains of meals taken, in short, no indication that a man has lived out in the wilds, watching his prey. Not so much as a soiled collar or some crumbs of bread.'

We had no difficulty in locating the search party, which gave me little hope of success in their venture, for surely their quarry could see their torches and hear their cries also. As my companion did not wish to be disturbed by conversation, I passed the time studying our fellows on the search. Holmes insists that I am in incurable dog-lover, and it is true that the barking of a large wolfhound - which I had no difficulty in identifying as the Scullions' beloved Finbarr - caught my attention. The man who struggled to hold onto Finbarr's leash, I could not immediately place. After a moment, though, I let out a self-deprecating laugh.

'I would not call myself a snob,' I said to Holmes, 'but it is odd that I did not recognise Seabury without his uniform.'

'Seabury?' Holmes repeated.

'Oh yes, Mr Holmes.' Merriman had managed to sneak up on us without a sound. I overcame my desire to start at the sound of his voice. 'All of Mr Scullion's male staff are here. He was quite insistent upon it.'

As we stepped aside to allow the sergeant to pass, I

recognised on Holmes' face that tense, faraway expression I associated with the highest manifestations of his genius.

'Am I growing old, Watson,' he asked, 'or has God reclaimed any brains he once saw fit to give me? What on earth is that infernal din?'

I shielded my eyes against an approaching light, but had I not done so, I should still have recognised the sound of an automobile engine. Improbable as it seemed, someone was driving a motor vehicle with considerable difficulty over the uneven surface of Mithering Woods. It came to an abrupt shuddering halt and a small, bearded man, leapt out and gazed accusingly at us.

'Mr Cadwallader!' Holmes cried, jovially. 'What a very pleasant surprise to see you again so soon!'

'Not so pleasant as all that, I assure you,' grumbled the lawyer. His twitches were now quite uncontrollable. 'You had no intention of following me to Norborough, did you, Mr Holmes?'

Holmes turned to me. 'Watson, did you forget to send that telegram?'

'Cease this tomfoolery, gentlemen! Answer me this: are you any closer to capturing Gideon Scullion's murderer?'

'Mr Merriman hopes very shortly to introduce you to him,' Holmes responded, pointing out the shamefaced sergeant with a wave of his stick.

'Not so soon as all that, Aldous,' said Merriman. 'I fear we will have to abandon the search. We are losing the light. Gentlemen, may I have your attention, please!'

At that moment, a shot rang out from somewhere deep in the woods. A cry of exultation spread through the group, and as one they surged forward, the lawyer and the policeman caught up in the excitement.

I found that a powerful hand gripping my shoulder tightly held me back. The hand belonged to Sherlock Holmes.

'We must go at once, Watson,' he said. 'I fear that I have made a terrible mistake.'

'I marvel at your expertise with this machine, Watson.'
While I relished the compliment, I felt I had to inform
Holmes that my wife's son, Elias, was part-owner of a
factory in which automobiles were manufactured. On the
occasion of my marriage to his mother, he had made me a
present of just such a vehicle. It had certainly proven of
great assistance when visiting housebound patients, and
was essential now as we sped towards Orlando Park.
'Can this apparatus go no faster? We have not a moment to
lose!'
'Holmes, why are we in such haste?' I asked, impatiently.
'Can it be that you do not see? So long as the search for
the Huntsman continues, Ambrose Scullion remains
unprotected!'
'Great Scott!' I cried. 'Then that was the sole reason for
the construction of the den.'
'Not the sole, Watson, but for the present it will suffice.'

The large house at Orlando Park was in total darkness as
we arrived. I feared that we had come too late and, as the
doors opened easily at his push, it was clear to me that
Holmes' thoughts were as mine.
'Search the rooms on the ground floor; I will look
upstairs,' he hissed. 'Go carefully, Watson.'
As I watched Holmes depart, I inwardly cursed the fact
that I had gone unarmed on one of our excursions for the
first time since the Field House affair of 1894. I had
ventured some way down the main corridor when I
became aware of sounds emanating from behind the door
at the very end of the passageway. I tensed myself as the
door swung open to reveal Ambrose Scullion, in nightshirt
and cap, holding a plate on which rested a large piece of
cheese.
'Who's there, I say! Who's there?' he barked.
I turned with a gasp, realising that Scullion was directing

his question to someone behind me. From the small amount of moonlight permitted by the open doors, I could make out a tall, rangy figure carrying what could only be a hunting rifle. In the split second I had to make my choice, I decided that Scullion was closer to me than the Huntsman, and so I bounded for the confused old man. The rugby skills of my Blackheath days had not deserted me, for I tackled him to the ground, just as a shot went off above our heads, dislodging a stuffed owl from its perch.

'Watson!' It was Sherlock Holmes, descending the stairs at a considerable rate. 'For the Lord's sake, Watson, say you are not injured!'

'I am quite well, Holmes,' I replied, as I shook sand from my fingers, 'just a little shaken, as is Mr Scullion. But the Huntsman, has he escaped?'

Holmes vanished through the doors for a few moments, before returning to us pale and harassed.

'Confound it!' he muttered, as we helped the dazed Scullion to his feet. 'There is little more that can be done tonight. Watson, I suggest that you remain here with Mr Scullion. I have no doubt that Sergeant Merriman and Aldous Cadwallader will arrive shortly on the trail of a stolen automobile. I will deal with them, and return to *The Prancing Pony* for the remainder of a night's sleep. I fully expect tomorrow to be a momentous day.'

I arrived at the inn the next morning just as Holmes was finishing off his breakfast. Mr Smallwood, who was removing his plate at that moment, looked up as I entered.

'Watson, where have you been?' Holmes asked. 'There is much to do today. I intend first to speak to Mr Scullion once more. There are one or two questions-'

'You will not see him,' I said, solemnly. 'Ambrose Scullion died last night.'

Both Holmes and Smallwood seemed shaken by the news.

'Died!' my friend repeated, hoarsely. 'How?'

'His weak constitution finally gave out under the stress of these terrible events.'

Holmes lowered his head. 'Then I have failed. The Huntsman has claimed his final victim, albeit indirectly, and has doubtless already fled the district. Come, Watson, we must pack our things and return to London. I do not wish to remain in Mithering a moment longer than is necessary. Mr Smallwood, would you be so good as to provide us with a bill? As soon as you are able, please, for I am in some haste to be away.'

It was a matter of only a few minutes for us to have our things packed away, ready for travel. As we passed the bar, Smallwood handed Holmes the bill for our food and accommodation. My friend studied it intently.

'Most interesting,' he said. 'Even when disguised, your handwriting betrays itself. There are several points of similarity between the sample you have been good enough to provide and the Huntsman's letters. I believe that I might make a credible witness for the prosecution, were I called upon to testify on the matter.'

The landlord went quite white. 'I do not know what you mean, Mr Holmes.'

'Please, Mr Scullion, let us not prolong this charade any longer, to do so would be both wearisome and profitless.'

I thought I had misheard. 'Holmes, did you call him "Mr Scullion"?'

'I am afraid there has not been sufficient time to acquaint you fully with the details of the case, Watson. Our host is none other than John Scullion, nephew of our client, who survived the train crash in Alabama.'

'Mr Holmes speaks the truth, doctor,' Smallwood replied, his composure having returned. He calmly walked out from behind the bar and took a seat at a nearby table.

'You are the last surviving heir,' I breathed.

'Not the last, Watson,' said Holmes. 'I see no need for you

to remain out there for the remainder of this discussion, Mrs Smallwood. Or would you prefer to be addressed by your given name of Miss Evelyn Scullion?'

The woman who had served our food the previous evening, appeared from the back room, brandishing a rifle. 'You are as clever as Dr Watson's stories claim,' she said.

'I understand that your late father was possessed of a somewhat eccentric disposition. Doubtless, he considered it amusing to pass his own name on to his daughter, not his son.'

'You are quite correct, Mr Holmes,' she replied, coolly. 'I was christened Evelyn Scullion.'

Holmes turned to face me. 'I have read that twins of opposite sexes are never identical, but there is nevertheless a strong family resemblance. I commented upon it when we arrived, never realising what it signified. When I saw Ambrose Scullion for the first time, I began to have some inkling of the truth.'

I moaned. 'And to think, I attributed his gauntness to his loss of will to live!'

'One can hardly blame old Ambrose for assuming that John and Evelyn were both boys. He never met them, and had little knowledge of them before their supposed deaths.'

'Do you know the meaning of the term "Doppelgänger", gentlemen?' Evelyn asked.

'It means "double", does it not?' I replied, desperately trying to catch Holmes' eye.

'Not quite, doctor,' she responded, her lips forming a cruel smile. 'A doppelgänger is the spirit of a still-living person. Don't you think that funny? We were dead to him, why should he not be dead to us?'

'Please, madam, do not attempt to suggest that your crimes concern anything other than your uncle's fortune.'

'We were raised in Long Island by a kindly but foolish couple, the Caves,' John Scullion volunteered. 'But we never forgot who we truly were. Eventually, we were able to amass sufficient proofs of our identity.'

'Whereupon, you came to England and learned that only two persons stood between you and a considerable sum of money,' Holmes added. 'Your enquiries hereabouts revealed that two strangers were about to enter Mithering, the Smallwoods. You waylaid, murdered, and replaced them.'

'Who would know the difference?' asked Evelyn, scornfully.

'I, for one. Your culinary skills are somewhat lacking for an innkeeper's wife.'

'Tom Smallwood's brother, for another' I suggested. 'His arrival took you by surprise, and he had to be killed also.'

'After he had been tortured in an attempt to discover whether your scheme had been jeopardised. His murder provided you with the ideal justification for leaving the district in haste, which you would have done in any case once Ambrose succumbed. We now know why you did not deliver the letter until after the murder of Gideon Scullion. A servant might easily have discarded it without a second thought before the crime occurred. But once young Scullion was dead, there was little danger of such a missive being ignored. And thus was the myth of the Huntsman created, giving the impression that this was an act of vengeance rather than a matter of succession. Murdering young Gideon first helped to muddy the waters also. If Ambrose Scullion had died naturally as was expected, all might have gone as intended. I am curious to know how your plan would have unfolded had it been successful.'

'We would have returned to the States and established our claim to Uncle's fortune through our lawyer,' Evelyn responded. 'Or should I say our solicitor? But it is successful, Mr Holmes. Only the two of you know the truth, and that inconvenience is easily removed.' She raised the weapon to fire.

'I urge you not to do anything precipitate, Miss Scullion. If you look to your left, you will observe that Sergeant Merriman has a similar firearm aimed directly at your head. I have no doubt that if he were to check your guest rooms, he would discover that one bed has been stripped of its linen, in order to provide a covering for the imaginary Huntsman's equally imaginary lair.'

Miss Scullion's jaw dropped, and the rifle sagged noticeably in her arms.

'I have, in the past, commented upon Dr Watson's commendable lack of guile, but I must congratulate him upon his performance this morning. Incidentally, you may both be interested to know that Ambrose Scullion, though a desperately ill man, still lives, and will no doubt be present when you are hanged.'

The little which I had yet to learn of this affair was told to me by Sherlock Holmes as we travelled back to London that evening. 'Why, I wondered, was Smallwood's body discovered so near the Huntsman's lair? Why did he not move the corpse to another part of the forest, allowing his hiding place to remain undiscovered? It has long been one of my maxims that when a fact appears to be opposed to a long train of deductions it invariably proves to be capable of some other interpretation. The absence of any traces of occupation in the warren told me that it was meant to be found. The twins made a virtue - or whatever the diabolical equivalent may be – out of a necessity following the murder of an unwelcome visitor who could unmask them as impostors. The construction of the Hunstman's lair served a triple purpose: It gave the impression that James Smallwood happened upon the Huntsman accidentally, it suggested that said Huntsman was to be found somewhere in the woods rather than in plain sight, and it set in motion the great hunt, which I am certain was suggested to our ambitious sergeant by John Scullion. Through the hunt, the populace were suitably distracted while the attack on Ambrose was staged.'

'John was present at the hunt,' I said, with increasing horror, 'so it must have been his sister, Evelyn, who made the attempt on her uncle's life!'

'While her brother fired the shot in the woods that caused so much confusion. You will recall that Merriman was on the brink of calling a halt to proceedings.'

'But why wait until that late hour to strike at old Ambrose?'

'The identities the Scullions had adopted in Mithering served them well in many respects, but they posed a major inconvenience in that they were expected to man the bar at *The Prancing Pony*. Thomas Smallwood could hardly be expected not to join the quest for his brother's killer. His sister had therefore to serve the inn's few customers before setting out upon her deadly mission.'

'Ambrose Scullion's choice of a quotation from *Hamlet* was an apt one; in a short time, the entire family will be dead.'

'I do not hold such sensational literature in high regard, Watson. I find the works of Mr Massinger considerably more agreeable.'

He did not speak again on the matter. Some hours later he muttered to himself 'Ghosts! Ghosts!', but what he meant by this, I never discovered.

THE ADVENTURE OF THE FORGETFUL
ASSASSIN

When leafing through my accounts of the adventures of
Sherlock Holmes, I find details of no less than 47 cases,
which, even at this late date, seem unlikely ever to be
released to the public. Several, including the curious
matter of Colonel James Moriarty and the scandalous
affair of the politician, the lighthouse and the trained
cormorant, I am barred from relating by legal obstructions.
Others are simply of too delicate a nature to be revealed
for fear of causing embarrassment to any of the
participants or their heirs. Indeed, it was only with the
recent death of Miss Susan Cushing that I was released
from my promise not to publish an account of her
grotesque and unsettling experience.
There is but one case that I have withheld for the sake of
my own feelings. However, recent remarks made by
certain of those individuals who purport to be admirers of
my writings have made it unavoidable. I refer to those
enthusiasts who indulge in what I believe is referred to as
"the game"; namely, perpetuating the fantasy that the
published extracts from the life of Sherlock Holmes are
nothing more than an elaborate fiction concocted by my
literary agent. In the past I have allowed such juvenilia to
go unchecked, but I have been prompted to take action by
a recent article in which it is alleged that a reference to my
good friend Charles Thurston in one of my earlier
reminiscences was intended as little more than a thinly-
disguised advertisement for a firm of billiard-table
manufacturers. It is only because I have no desire to see
his memory sullied unnecessarily that I am at last relating
the particulars concerning his demise, though there
remains much about the affair that I have cause to regret –
most of all, my passionate quarrel with Holmes over the
pertinacity with which he conducted his enquiry. But the

facts are always preferable to idle and grossly inaccurate speculation.

After so many years at Holmes' side I should, one imagines, be used to sudden incursion into our mundane existence by the tragic and dramatic, but of all our investigations, I find that I cannot describe the events of that day in the February of 1901 without what a more fanciful person might describe as a sense of dread. Finding that my fellow lodger's love of companionable silence had ceased to be companionable, I had had decided to visit my club where, over more than a few brandies than is perhaps advisable, I passed the time in the company of several old acquaintances, among them Julian Emery, Gideon Makepeace and Charles Thurston. So agreeable was the experience that I invited Thurston to return with me to Baker Street, where I could regale him with further tales of our many triumphs.

Beyond an initial handshake, Holmes paid no attention to Thurston or I, preferring instead to rearrange the items on his chemistry table. But a man of Holmes' stature and personality cannot be easily ignored, even when he works in silence. I suspect that Thurston may have grown uncomfortable in Holmes' presence, for he twice asked me to explain the solution to the Camberwell poisoning case. 'Once Holmes knew the victim had gone to bed within two hours of winding his watch,' I repeated, 'the case became as clear as crystal. A child could have worked it out.'
'Not your child, Watson!' he guffawed. I joined in, for I knew Thurston's good-natured ribbing of old.
Holmes cleared his throat loudly.
'You remember the Camberwell poisoning case, don't you, Holmes?'
Pretending that he had not been paying attention, the

detective raised his head. 'Hm? I'm sorry, Watson, what were you saying?'

I felt certain that he was fully aware of the body of our conversation, but I nevertheless explained that I had been entertaining Thurston with the story of our most notable coup. 'Quite a pretty little problem, eh?'

'I prefer to think of it as an instructive exercise in logical deduction.'

Clearly sensing the coldness in Holmes' reply, Thurston rose from his chair and began to don his hat and coat.

'Well, either way, it was a rattling good yarn! And now I must be off, I'm afraid. Harley Street beckons. Mr Holmes?' He gave an informal salute, and received a nod of the head in return.

As we descended the stairs, I asked Thurston what he had meant when he mentioned Harley Street. 'Nothing serious, I hope?'

'Something very serious, Watters, old man – money! Half those medicos owe their gold cuff links to my advice. I say, I don't suppose you could talk Holmes into sinking a little capital into San Pedro tin?'

I laughed as I opened the door for him. 'I doubt that very much. I expect that he would say he has sufficient for his needs.'

'How very peculiar,' replied Thurston. '"More" has always been *my* favourite amount! Well, good-day to you!'

As I returned to the sitting-room, I pondered whether I should refrain from commenting upon Holmes' apparent rudeness, but when I discovered him lounging in the chair so recently vacated by Thurston, I found I had to speak.

'Is it really too much to ask for a little common civility, Holmes?' I asked. 'This is my home as well as your workplace.'

Holmes expression was one of innocent incomprehension. 'You are quite welcome to play host to whomever you

54

wish – my dear Watters.'

Where I had taken Thurston's ragging in good humour, I was now profoundly aggravated. I opened my mouth to speak, but whatever my reply would have been, it is now lost to my memory. For at that moment, the ghastliest cry I have ever heard reached us from the street below. In my capacity as a physician as well as that of assistant to Holmes, I fear that I have heard many screams of agony through the years. But this was all the more horrifying for the fact that I recognised the voice as that of Charles Thurston.

We rushed downstairs, and I flung open the door to be confronted by a mass of onlookers. I fought my way through the crowd, but it was far too late for any assistance; Thurston lay dead at the foot of our steps, blood spilling from a deep wound in his chest. I heard an aggravated grunt and realised that the gap in the wall of gawkers had closed behind me, and that Holmes was struggling to emerge. I looked about me in the faint hope that I might catch a glimpse of the party responsible for this terrible attack. To my amazement, my hopes were rewarded, for I observed a tall, thin young man clad in a long overcoat turn his back upon the spectacle and begin to depart. It was clear from the unnatural way he kept his right arm close to his side that he was attempting to hide something about his person. In an instant, I had risen and begun my pursuit. My quarry seemed at first confused, but realising that I was dogging his steps, he broke into a run. His long legs might have seen him halfway across Blandford Street had he not been hampered by the need to hold onto the murder weapon. My fury kept my own legs moving beyond the point where the pain of my old wound might ordinarily have forced me to stop. I wrestled the young man to the ground, placing sufficient pressure upon his arm that he was forced to drop the knife – it was a long thin blade, and seemed curiously familiar. But my anger was too great at that moment to permit me to take in all its details. My captive's bowler hat came off in the struggle, and grabbing a fistful of ginger hair, I pressed his face into the grime of the street. I dread to think what act my rage might have led me to perpetrate, had not Holmes arrived at that moment.

'Watson!' he cried. 'Watson, are you all right?'

At the sound of his voice, the spell was broken, and I felt in a rush all the agony I had blotted out in my desire to capture Thurston's killer.

'I'm- quite all right- Holmes,' I gasped, though in truth I felt far from well. I attempted to rouse my prisoner, but he remained a dead weight upon the pavement. With Holmes, assistance, I was able to turn the fellow over. He was fully conscious: a man of about five and twenty years, with a narrow face and lank red hair. But in his blue eyes, I saw no comprehension whatsoever.

Despite Mrs Hudson's insistence that I remain at Baker Street and submit myself to her ministrations, I was insistent upon discovering all I could about this dazed madman who had murdered my friend. Inspector Lestrade, who had been placed in charge of the case, was, of course, only too glad of our assistance. So it was that we three were in a cell at the Bow Street station some hours later, as the prisoner began to stir from his curious waking slumber. He stared at us in turn, before focussing upon his surroundings. 'What- what *is* this place?' he murmured. 'Where am I?'

'You're in the Bow Street cells,' Lestrade replied. 'Now, what's your name?'

The young man considered this for a moment. 'My name is Alexander Hydell. Have I been arrested for something?'

'"Something", he says! Only murder, my lad!'

It was not my place to participate in an interrogation, but I could not remain silent. 'Why did you kill Charles

Thurston?' I asked, harshly.

'Who are you?' Hydell asked in reply.

'Never mind who he is, just answer his question,' Lestrade ordered.

'I've never heard of Charles Thurston.'

The inspector raised his arms to the heavens as though imploring the almighty for patience. 'Ah, the old sweet song! So you don't remember a thing about it? Don't remember stabbing Mr Charles Thurston, a respected member of the London business community, through the heart on the steps of number 221B Baker Street?'

Dark though it was, I was aware for the first time of some dawning realization in the young man's features.

'No, I didn't- I mean, I remember killing- I'm not sure.'

'Fascinating,' said Holmes, the first word he had uttered since we had entered the cell.

'The knife we took off you looks like something a doctor might use,' said Lestrade. 'You don't look much like a doctor to me.'

'I'm not a doctor, I'm a shipping clerk,' Hydell protested. 'I told you, my name is Alexander Hydell, I live on Bolton Street and I've never heard of anyone called Thurston!'

'I'm not interested in your life story, I want to know where you got the knife!'

'I don't remember,' was the sulky reply. Hydell curled up into a ball and lay with his back to us. Lestrade simply sighed. I have never claimed to be a professional detective, but I fancy that after two decades' worth of investigations, I can tell when a person is concealing something. I saw it then, and I had no doubt that it was an admission of guilt.

When it became clear that we would learn nothing more from the killer, Holmes asked that he be allowed to examine the murder weapon. Lestrade led us to his office, a tiny room with a huge ledger upon the table, and a telephone projecting from the wall. He removed the knife gingerly from a drawer, and passed it to Holmes, knowing better than to remind my friend of the importance of handling evidence with care.

Holmes studied the long-bladed weapon minutely.

'Watson, this is more in your line, I think.' Observing my distracted manner, he added, 'If you feel up to it, that is.'

'It's quite all right, Holmes,' I told him. 'It's called a bistoury. It's a surgical instrument. Hasn't been sharpened in many years.' I refrained from observing that it had, however, been sharp enough to kill Charles Thurston.

'It's distressing when an implement meant to save lives is used to take them,' Holmes mused. 'The blade is the finest Sheffield steel, Thomas Firth and Sons, if I'm not mistaken. The engraving on the handle is specific to Featherstone's of Knightsbridge. This was therefore an order for a well-to-do customer – a former surgeon.'

'Why not a practising surgeon?' Lestrade asked.

Holmes shook his head. 'Why would the owner allow the tools of his trade to get into this condition unless he no longer practised surgery? It should be a simple enough matter for you to trace the owner, Lestrade.'

The necessity of this task eluded me; With Hydell in custody, I could not see how it mattered how he came by the knife. The Inspector voiced the same objection.

Holmes was unperturbed. 'Yes, but it would be interesting to discover, would it not, how the bistoury passed from the hands of a wealthy former surgeon to those of a working-class shipping clerk from Bolton Street? As you say, Inspector, the killer is behind bars. What harm could it do to satisfy my curiosity?'

Holmes' prediction was correct; the manager of Featherstone's, an efficient if somewhat aloof gentleman by the name of Davison, had no difficulty in identifying the owner of the bistoury.

'Ah yes,' he announced in strident tones. 'A somewhat out of the ordinary request. Usually, you know, we deal in fine cutlery. If any of you gentlemen are looking for a suitable purchase for a wedding or anniversary, might I suggest..? No? Well, in any case, I think I can say with all modesty that we rose to the challenge on this occasion. Yes, Dr Saunders was most satisfied with his purchase.'

I found it hard to fathom as we stood in the elegantly-appointed Harley Street consulting rooms of Dr Felix Saunders, that the incident that set us on this erratic trail – the murder of Charles Thurston – had occurred only hours before.

Lestrade let out a whistle as he examined our opulent surroundings. 'Business must be good,' he observed, 'whatever business is.'

'His official title is "psychoanalyst,"' Holmes replied, holding up the business card he had taken from the salver in the hallway. The Inspector held out his hand, clearly wishing to examine the card for himself, but Holmes, apparently failing to notice our colleague's action, placed it in his top pocket.

Overlooking the apparent slight, Lestrade said, 'So this fellow's an alienist, then, like that German doctor?'

A booming voice from the doorway caused us all to turn our heads. '"That German doctor" is Moravian, and his name is Freud'.

Doctor Felix Saunders presented a gargantuan figure, his craggy and deeply seamed face and fierce eyes could not fail to hold the attention. His enormous beard was as grey as the flakes of cigar ash that spotted his waistcoat.

Holmes appeared unaffected by the entrance of our impressive host. 'Tell me, Dr Saunders, is the term "psychoanalyst" your own, or of Freud's devising?'

The doctor raised a quizzical eyebrow. 'You're unusually inquisitive for a policeman', said he. 'Does it really take

three of you to return a missing instrument?
I could hardly fail to take note of the significance of this
remark. 'A *surgical* instrument?' I enquired.
'I was not referring to a musical instrument,' Saunders
replied, leaving me feeling somewhat foolish. 'I reported it
missing some days ago. Dare I take it you've found it at
last? What became of Sergeant Rance, by the way?'
Lestrade stepped forward and introduced himself.
Saunders seemed unimpressed, as though a fly had
attempted to disturb a deity. 'I'd like to ask you a few
questions about Alexander Hydell,' the inspector
continued.
A moment passed in silence, as though Saunders were
considering how best to respond. 'Well, Inspector,' he
said, 'I can spare you a few minutes before my next
appointment. I hope you won't take it amiss if I don't ask
you to be seated. Are these gentlemen also police officers?
They seem a little old to be your underlings.'
Holmes smiled. 'We strive in our small way to support
justice, Sir. My name is Sherlock Holmes this is my
colleague, Dr Watson.'
'Indeed? I always thought you were imaginary, Mr
Holmes, like Father Christmas. Well, what is it that you
wish to know about Hydell? I need hardly point out that I
will most likely be bound by the rules of confidentiality
governing my profession.'
'Hydell *is* your patient, then?' I asked.
'He is. What about him?'
'He murdered a man named Charles Thurston earlier
today, using your stolen bistoury,' I replied, bluntly.
If I had expected some response akin to shock from
Saunders, I was to be disappointed. 'Well, well,' was all he
had to say.
'Were you acquainted with Mr Thurston?' Lestrade
enquired.
Saunders gave a shrug of his massive shoulders. 'I doubt if

there's a doctor on Harley Street who hasn't had dealings with Mr Thurston.' I recollected my friend's parting words as I saw him onto Baker Street: 'Half those medicos owe their gold cuff-links to my advice'. I looked to Holmes, wondering what he might make of the interview, but to my surprise, he seemed less interested in our impressive host than in the contents of his bookshelves.

'When did you report the theft of the knife?' asked the inspector.

'I would prefer it if you referred to the instrument by its correct name, Mr Lestrade; I reported the theft of the bistoury last Friday.'

'And did you see Mr Hydell on that day?'

'Last Wednesday, actually. But it was only by chance that I happened to notice the theft. When I changed fields six years ago, I cleaned my surgical instruments and put the case in that cabinet. I rarely have call to look in it these days. It was mere chance that I did so on Friday. And before you ask, no, I do not normally keep it locked. Doubtless that was naïve of me. You may rest assured that I have since taken the appropriate precautions.'

It struck me that Saunders' arrogant manner seemed entirely at odds with his chosen profession. I shuddered inwardly at the thought of spending even an hour in his company socially, let alone as a patient.

Holmes' attention returned, at last, to the matter at hand. 'From the little I have seen of Alexander Hydell,' he commented, 'he does not appear to be the sort of man who could meet your fees, Doctor. How, then, did he come to be your patient?'

'I don't- *didn't* charge Hydell for his treatment. He was referred by a colleague, Dr Reginald Ward. I have no truck, you see, with the modern preoccupation for leisure pursuits. I fill my remaining time treating those who cannot otherwise afford my somewhat expensive services.'

I began to think better of Saunders. Perhaps, I thought, I

had allowed his apparent pomposity to blind me to his finer qualities.

'So, as a psycho... *analyst*,' Lestrade struggled with the term, 'you treat patients who are going 'round the twist. So tell me, Dr Saunders: how far 'round the twist was Hydell?'

'I find that a very vulgar and insensitive remark, Inspector,' the doctor grumbled, 'and I prefer not to answer questions regarding my patients.'

'And do your medical ethics stretch to a patient who is deceased?'

Saunders gave this point a moment's thought. 'That, of course, would be a different matter.'

'Well, in a very short space of time, your Mr Hydell will be hanged for murder.'

'Then come back when you've hanged him and we'll talk again.' I was quite taken aback by the callousness of Saunders' response. Perhaps I had, after all, been over-generous in assuming that he was possessed of an altruistic nature, unless he kept it uncommonly well-concealed.

'Really, gentlemen, I fail to see why you are wasting your time and, more importantly, mine. Clearly, Hydell stole the bistoury when I was out of the room, and then used it to kill Thurston for his own reasons.'

Holmes spoke up. 'Hydell's recollections of the incident are unusually vague. And unlike you, Doctor, he claims not to have known Mr Thurston.' Saunders would not be drawn on this point. He and the detective locked eyes.

'I wonder,' Holmes went on, apparently unaffected by the obvious tension, 'if you practice hypnosis on your patients? I notice several volumes about hypnotism on your bookcase, including one by Franz Mesmer himself. I envy you your collection.'

'Envy is the beginning of all true greatness, Mr Holmes. Am I to understand that you are of the opinion that Mr

Hydell may have been instructed to kill Thurston under hypnosis?'

'Is it possible?'

'Not remotely,' Saunders replied, scornfully. 'Such notions exist only in the minds of authors of yellow-backed fiction.'

'Then what explanation do you have for Alexander Hydell's murderous attack upon a total stranger, Doctor? Or would that explanation breach medical ethics?'

With great care, Saunders removed a fat cigar from the box on his well-polished desk. 'Are you any of you, by chance, familiar with the condition known as Poriomania?' he asked.

Although I have never treated a patient suffering from that malady, I did indeed recognise the term. I explained to my colleagues that Poriomania is a cognitive function disorder in which the sufferer can behave in a certain way without having any recollection of his actions. Saunders seemed profoundly unimpressed by my display of medical knowledge.

'And did you diagnose Alexander Hydell as suffering from Poriomania?' I asked.

'I did not, but I venture to suggest that it would explain his behaviour. He kills Charles Thurston during one of these blackouts; naturally his memories of the event would be hazy.'

I considered this. A diagnosis of Poriomania might well account for Hydell's violent behaviour. It might even save him from the noose, although, to my shame, I had at that moment no real interest in seeing him escape retribution for Thurston's murder.

A ring of the doorbell brought the discussion to an end. 'My next patient, gentlemen,' Saunders observed. 'I take it you have nothing else?'

'I don't believe so, no,' Lestrade replied. 'Well, thank-you for your time, Dr Saunders, and thank-you for that

63

suggestion about the Porio- er... Thank-you, Doctor.'

I was quite satisfied that matters should be left as they
stood for the remainder of the day, and Lestrade expressed
his opinion that we should consider our work done. If
Alexander Hydell was indeed prone to a condition that
caused him to act in a fashion he could not later recollect,
then perhaps Dr Saunders could be persuaded to visit the
young man in his cell and verify that diagnosis. Holmes,
however, was quite insistent that we speak to Hydell at the
earliest opportunity. Lestrade capitulated, but wishing to
have nothing further to do with the matter, retreated to his
minuscule office, leaving us to conduct the interrogation.
I was uneasy at the thought that Holmes might bring up
the subject of Dr Saunders' methods during the discussion.
I had little sympathy for Hydell's plight, but I felt that
such an approach would hardly be ethical. I was
particularly perturbed by Holmes' suggestion that Hydell
might have been instructed to murder Thurston while
under hypnosis.
'It is a fruitless line of enquiry,' I advised him, as the
uniformed officer unlocked the cell door for us. 'A person
cannot be made to perform an act that is contrary to their
will or nature, especially murder.'
'A pity,' was all that Sherlock Holmes had to say before
we entered.
Rocking back and forth on his cot, Alexander Hydell
seemed more pathetic than before. He would not raise his
head to meet my gaze. I was troubled to observe several
clumps of reddish hair on the floor of the cell, as though
he had torn them from his own scalp in frustration.
'You again,' he muttered, more to himself than for our
benefit.
'Mr Hydell,' Holmes began, making no attempt to ease the
man's misery, 'your own physician referred you to Dr
Felix Saunders for treatment – why?'

64

Alexander Hydell let out a long sigh and stretched out on the cot. 'I've always found it difficult to keep a job, Mr Holmes,' he said, 'or my temper. There was a woman in my life. Lily. We were to be married. But my dark moods became too much for her. I thought if I could just find a cure for my anger, I might win her back'

'And what form did Dr Saunders' treatment take?'

'He was very interested in my dreams about my uncle,' Hydell replied, eventually. 'He and my father were brothers, partners in a successful glassware firm in Manchester. When I was very small, Uncle Maurice forced his own brother out of the business. Dad took me with him to London to try and start a new life down here.'

'What had become of your mother?' I asked, unable to restrain my own curiosity.

'She died when I was a baby. My father was never able to rebuild his fortune, and he died a bitter and broken man. The Doctor seemed to think that might have been the start of it all. I really don't remember.'

'And in order to remedy this condition, did Dr Saunders ever place you in a hypnotic trance?' Holmes enquired. I cleared my throat loudly, but he chose to disregard my interruption.

'He… said it would help ease my nerves.' To my surprise, an unpleasant, almost vicious grin began to spread on the young prisoner's features.

'And what is so amusing?' I asked, unable to disguise my distaste.

'I was just thinking… it's funny. In all my dreams, my uncle always looks the same. Same clothes, same expression on his face. I haven't seen him since I was a boy, so I only know him from an old picture I keep in my rooms. Funny.'

Holmes' face flushed and darkened. His brows were drawn into two hard, black lines, while his eyes shone out from beneath them with a steely glitter. He placed his palm on my shoulder, indicating that it was time for us to leave. With his other hand, he knocked on the cell door. I heard the key turning on the other side.

'I'm sure we shall speak again, Mr Hydell,' was all Holmes said as we departed.

The prisoner gave no reply.

Silence reigned as we made our way back to Lestrade's office. The Inspector sat with feet propped up on his desk, reading *The Mystery of a Hansom Cab*. At our entrance, he made a futile attempt to hide the volume, but then relaxed upon discovering that we were not of the official force.

'Well, gentlemen,' he said with a sigh, 'did you get what you came for?'

I, for one, did not know how to answer this question, since I had not been entirely sure *what* we had come for; Holmes did not give a direct reply, choosing instead to answer Lestrade's question with a question of his own.

'Inspector, if you saw one man shoot another in public, would you then arrest the bullet?'

The policemen shot a baffled gaze in my direction. 'Do you know what he's on about, Doctor?'

I shook my head.

'Would it be fair to say,' Holmes continued, 'that I have, on occasion, been of some assistance to you in your investigations?'

'I'd say that was something of an understatement, Mr Holmes,' the policeman replied with disarming honesty.

'We might say that the slate had been wiped clean if you were to do something for me now. It is no small thing, you understand, but I feel certain that the results will prove worthwhile. Oh, Watson, would you be so good as to hail a cab for us? I shan't be more than a few minutes longer.'

I had long since grown accustomed to Holmes' intentionally mysterious nature – he was exceedingly loath to communicate his full plans until the instant of their fulfilment - but I felt certain that I was being sent out of earshot for fear that I might take objection to the request he was about to make. As I flagged down a cab, I felt my anger growing, but I was determined to prevent it from rising to the surface. To give voice to such strong emotions would be to create unnecessary discord, and though my nerves had long since settled following my Afghan experiences, I still retained an abhorrence of rows.

I resisted the temptation to question Holmes about the case on the journey back to Baker Street, but upon our arrival, I found I could no longer hold my tongue.

'Well, Holmes, do I take it your investigation is not at an end?' I asked.

'The faculty for deduction must be contagious,' he observed, lighting a cigarette. 'You are correct, Watson. Dr Felix Saunders knows a good deal more than he is telling.'

While I had been very far from impressed by Saunders' haughty manner, I saw nothing underhanded in his diagnosis.

Holmes threw himself into his armchair. 'I wish I could share your bland appraisal of the matter, old fellow. Like Da Vinci, however, I am a disciple of experience. Is it reasonable that Hydell should have been left alone in his consulting room long enough to be able to locate, steal and conceal the bistoury?'

'Holmes, you always say that once the impossible has been eliminated, whatever remains, however improbable, must be the truth. It may be improbable that Hydell should be left alone for a sufficient length of time, but it is hardly impossible. Surely Saunders' theory that Hydell suffers from Poriomania explains his unorthodox behaviour.'

He sent up a great blue triumphant cloud from his cigarette. 'On the contrary, Watson, that is the one point where his story falls down. As I have had occasion to remind you before, there is nothing more deceptive than an obvious fact. The theft of the bistoury indicates premeditation. We must look for consistency. Where it is lacking, we must suspect deception.'

'So it is your contention that Saunders provided Hydell with the bistoury. But surely that defies logic, since he must have known that such an unusual weapon could easily be traced back to him. And why then report its theft to the police?'

'A cunning stoke, that. He *wished* the blade to be traced, in order that he might feed us the notion that Hydell committed the murder during a mental blackout – a story, I might add, that both you and the Inspector lapped up. For shame, Watson.'

My anger welled up once more, and this time I had no desire to restrain it. 'But the mighty Sherlock Holmes wasn't fooled for a minute!' I cried. 'You really are a thinking machine, aren't you? Utterly bereft of emotion! We're not dealing with one of your "exercises in logical deduction", Holmes! This concerns the death of my friend! Lestrade has the man who killed him under lock and key! Why can't you see the hurt your stubbornness is causing?'

For a moment, Holmes appeared on the brink of defending his position with the same vigour, but then his features softened. His clear, hard eyes were dimmed. 'Watson, I beg of you, just give me one more day to complete my enquiries. If after that, I cannot prove my suspicions, I'll drop the matter entirely.'

I considered his offer and the manner in which it had been given. 'Do I have your word, then?'

'As a gentleman. And, I hope, as your friend.'

Nothing more was said of the matter that evening, though I spent little enough of it in Holmes' company, before retiring to my room, exhausted. I was not surprised to discover upon rising that Holmes had already departed – indeed, I doubted that he had slept at all. Where such exertions as we had undergone the day before would induce torpor in any normal man, he seemed somehow to draw strength from them. I found a note affixed to our mantelpiece by a jack-knife. It read: 'Watson – we are too conspicuous together at present. We must take separate paths. S.H.' I took leave to doubt his stated justification for his actions. After the argument of the night before, it was obvious to me that Holmes wished to work undisturbed by the possibility of further confrontation. Deducing that he had no desire for me to "take a separate path" in our present investigation, I spent the majority of my morning attempting to organise my notes of our recent cases. At lunchtime, Mrs Hudson announced the arrival of Inspector Lestrade. His face was flushed, and it was clear to me that he had some important information to relate. His expression became crestfallen upon discovering that Holmes had not yet returned.

'Our friend is a terrible timekeeper, Doctor,' he observed.

'He summoned you, then?'

'I received a telegram about an hour ago. There's nothing in it to tell me what he's up to, mind. He's inscrutable as a Chinaman when he chooses. If it weren't for the fact that he gets results, I swear…'

Lestrade was interrupted at that moment by Holmes' return. He was in high spirits, apparently oblivious to the violent dispute of the night before. His eyes were shining and his cheeks tinged with colour. Only at a crisis have I seen those battle-signals flying.

'Good afternoon, Inspector! Help yourself to a cigar, by all means.'

Lestrade gave a nod of acknowledgement as the detective dropped into his favourite chair with a noisy expression of relief.

'Ah, it's good to be off my feet after such a busy morning!'

'Are you ready to reveal what you have been up to, then?'

I asked.

'No mystery, Watson. I've been busy in the financial district. After that, I paid a visit to the Bolton Street home of the incarcerated Mr Hydell. A few sovereigns in the palm of his grasping landlady, Mrs Ecclestone, afforded me entrance to his modest apartment.'

'And did you find what you were looking for, Mr Holmes?'

'I am delighted to say that my search was entirely in vain, Lestrade.' It was clearly pointless to ask Holmes to elucidate at this time. He would reveal the meaning behind his veiled reply when he saw fit. 'And now, you are obviously bursting with news. Let us have it.'

'I'm sorry to have to tell you, Mr Holmes, that your plans have gone awry.' From the satisfaction in Lestrade's tone, I suspected that he was not truly sorry at all.

'How so?' asked Holmes.

'I telephoned the Manchester police as you requested. They had no trouble locating Maurice Hydell and persuading him to come down to London on the double.' Now, at least, I knew the nature of the favour Holmes had asked of his Scotland Yard crony. 'The prisoner didn't seem to recognise him at first, but as soon as the uncle introduced himself-'

'Alexander Hydell attacked him,' Holmes concluded, sententiously.

Lestrade was crestfallen to discover that Holmes had been anticipating this outcome all along, but he was not to be put off. 'It took three of us to prise his hands off the old feller's neck. This proves his guilt beyond doubt, I'd say.'

Holmes laughed softly to himself. 'My dear Inspector, it proves just the opposite, I should say. And now, if neither of you gentlemen has any pressing business within the next hour, perhaps you might accompany me on a little excursion, at the end of which I expect to introduce you to the person responsible for the murder of Charles

Thurston.'

'Really, gentlemen!' exclaimed Dr Saunders with exasperation. 'You must understand that I have a practice to run. You simply cannot monopolise my time like this.' Lestrade offered his apologies and nothing more, for he had no more notion than I of what had brought us back to the psychoanalyst's opulent Harley Street consulting room. 'I fear that your patients will have to do without your treatment from now on,' Holmes replied, casually.

The doctor took his cigar from his lips and gazed sternly at my companion. 'Because you expect to arrest me, perhaps? Be sure of your facts, Mr Holmes. Be very sure'

'Am I correct is saying, Doctor Saunders, that before you began a business association with Charles Thurston, your financial interests were dealt with by a Mr Foster Barrington?' The name Foster Barrington had a familiar ring to it, and I fancied that I might have seen it in Holmes' irregular index, under "F".

'I make no secret of the fact,' said Saunders. 'What of it?'

'Foster Barrington fled the country two years ago when certain improprieties in his business practices came to light. I suggest, Doctor, that you were in collusion with Barrington, and when you put your affairs in Thurston's hands, he discovered the illegalities and proceeded to blackmail you. I am most sorry, Watson, but I have no doubt that it is the truth.'

I was appalled at this suggestion, but Saunders' reaction was even more dramatic. His fierce face turned to a dusky red, his eyes glared, and the knotted, passionate veins started out in his forehead. 'Preposterous! Thurston was already a wealthy man and I was his paying client. Why on earth should he have wished to blackmail me?'

'Because, as I had occasion to overhear him say, "more" was his favourite amount.'

'A most astute and concise diagnosis, Mr Holmes.'

Holmes bowed his head in acknowledgement. 'In my years as a consulting detective I have gained some insight into human behaviour. You, for instance, strike me as a man who is nothing if not methodical and precise.'
Saunders bowed his own head in return.
'Why should it be, I wonder,' Holmes went on, 'that *your* fingerprints, as well as Hydell's, were on the bistoury when I examined it? Did you not tell us in this very room that you had cleaned your surgical instruments before putting them away?'
After the surprise of Holmes' initial accusation, the psychoanalyst was more guarded in his reactions. 'Forgive me, Mr Holmes, but since you have not taken my fingerprints for the purposes of making a comparison, I should have to say that you are lying.'
'They were on your business card, Doctor.' I recalled the careful manner in which Holmes had handled the card, and how he had prevented Lestrade from touching it. 'I ask again: how came your fingerprints onto the blade?'
Saunders gave a mighty shrug, and a large flake of ash dropped from his cigar and landed at his feet. 'I can only suggest, Holmes, that you have too high an estimate of my methodical and precise nature.'
'Please forgive me, but I would appreciate it if you would do me the honour of giving me my prefix, Doctor.' When Saunders said nothing, Holmes continued as though the moment had not occurred. 'I suggest that your fingerprints found their way onto the knife when, after placing him in a deep hypnotic trance, you handed it to Hydell in order to have him kill Thurston.'
I had been silent until that point I felt that I could not allow the interview to continue without voicing an objection. 'Holmes, I'm sorry, but that can't be – one cannot be induced to kill if it is not in one's nature!'
The detective nodded, sagely. 'How right you are, my dear Watson. But murder *is* in Hydell's nature; at least in

respect of one specific individual. Think.'

The answer came to me at the same moment it occurred to Lestrade. 'His Uncle!' the Inspector cried.

'Their dramatic reunion in the cells proves as much. Through your "charity work", Doctor, you found your ideal subject in Hydell and exploited his murderous resentment in order to turn him into a- well, a living weapon. I fancy you did not even have to give the order to kill; you simply persuaded him to transpose the face of his uncle with that of Thurston and told him where to be on a particular day so that he might see his target. His hatred for his long-lost relative did the rest. No doubt Hydell followed Thurston and Dr Watson from their club before laying in wait at Baker Street. A poor choice of address from your point of view, Dr Saunders, but in his mesmerized state, the young man could hardly be expected to show much discernment.'

The bristles below Saunders nose quivered with amusement. 'Mr Holmes, what an interesting patient you would make, you really are quite the fantasist. What a pity you have no proof! Only surmise and wild conjecture!'

For a moment, Sherlock Holmes appeared defeated, for it was quite true that he had no further argument to make that might support his theory. Then, quite unexpectedly, he observed: 'A tidy office is indicative of a tidy mind, Doctor, and your consulting room is extremely tidy. Not an item out of place. Save for that book.'

As one man, we all three turned to examine Saunders' bookcase. All the volumes were arranged with great care save for one, a treatise on hypnotism by Mesmer, which was out of line with its neighbours. Clearly, the owner had referred to it quite recently. Before the doctor could object, Holmes removed the book from the shelf.

'May I open it?' Holmes asked.

'You may not,' Saunders replied, curtly.

'Why not?'

'I do not wish it.'

'You'll have to do as the Doctor says, Mr Holmes,' Lestrade informed him. 'The book is his property after all.'

Seeming to acquiesce, Holmes held the tome out at arms' length. As Saunders went to snatch it, however, he allowed it to fall from his grasp. As the book landed, two photographs slid from its pages. Holmes was quick to retrieve them. A sardonic smile broke through his ascetic gloom.

'What have we here?' he asked. 'My carelessness has resulted in a most important find. Of course, I recognise the gentleman in this photograph as the late Mr Charles Thurston, but the other is unknown to me. I wonder... Lestrade, could you identify this individual?'

As Lestrade studied the photograph, recognition began to dawn on his features. 'He's bald now, and fatter round the middle, but yes, I saw him only today... This is Alexander Hydell's Uncle Maurice.'

I began dimly to realise what my friend was hinting at. The idea was both incredible and appalling, and yet it might be possible.

'I failed to find the photograph in Hydell's rooms this morning,' Holmes explained. 'Tell me, Doctor, did you instruct him under hypnosis to bring it to you? You would prefer not to say? No matter, it will be quite clear to a jury that you used these pictures when instructing Hydell that whenever he saw *this* man, Thurston, the face he imagined he saw would be *this* face, his hated uncle. Of course, it would have to be the photograph your patient has kept since childhood. He might not recognise his uncle as he is today. It took him some moments to do so, in fact, when I arranged a family reunion earlier today.'

'Think you're clever, don't you, Holmes?' Saunders growled.

'As a matter of fact, Doctor,' Holmes replied, 'I do.'

There remains little more to tell. Saunders' bombastic nature proved no match for the relentless interrogation of a Scotland Yard official, and he soon confessed to the scheme Holmes had outlined. Maurice Hydell returned to his native Manchester, bruised and shaken but not badly harmed. His troubled nephew was removed to an asylum, and it pains me to say that after all this time I have taken no steps to enquire after his condition. A man of exceptional evil cruelly exploited his illness, that much I know. But I will always carry with me the memory of a tall, thin young man in a long overcoat, fleeing from the murder of a man I choose to remember as a friend.

THE ADVENTURE OF THE HONOURABLE
CRACKSMAN

'I'm sorry, Watson, I cannot permit it.'
With these few words, Sherlock Holmes forbade me from
publishing the details of surrounding the grotesque tragedy
of Ham Common within the lifetime of any of the
participants. This despite the fact that, while not the
greatest example of his mental dexterity, it was perhaps
the game played for the highest stakes in his career up to
that point. But even the opportunity to relate to the public
the facts concerning the rematch against one of his
deadliest adversaries did not serve as an inducement, for
Holmes felt that any record of the matter could only
blacken the reputation of one whom he held in the highest
regard. And so I add this account to my increasingly
cramped dispatch-box, hoping that the story can one day
be told.

Owing to some small lapse in my note-taking at the time, I
am uncertain now as to the precise date, save that it was a
Tuesday, late in the year 1899.
'I am used, as a rule, to being consulted in these rooms,'
Holmes announced, as he examined the only item of
correspondence to arrive that morning. 'This, I fancy, is a
unique request. One can only hope that it is not the
beginning of a trend.'
'What does it say?' I asked.
'The sender, who does not give his name, wishes to meet
us in the steam rooms at the Olympia Baths. Ordinarily, I
would refuse such an extraordinary request out of hand,
but the London criminal has been such a dull dog of
late…'
'Listening could do no harm,' I remarked. In truth, the idea
of a Turkish bath appealed to me very much at that

moment, for I had been feeling rheumatic and old for some days.

'Your enthusiasm for this foreign luxury does you no credit, Watson,' Holmes smiled. 'Curious, that a potential client should be so reluctant to advertise.'

'What can be his purpose, do you think?'

'I cannot make bricks without clay, Doctor. We shan't know until we find ourselves at the Olympia.'

Holmes demanded consistency in his professional dealings, but his opinions on certain matters were apt to change from moment to moment. So it was with the subject of his bathing preferences. One week, he might criticise any red-blooded Englishman who would prefer to soothe his aching muscles in a Turkish bath, the next would find him relaxing at the Olympia, his previous objections forgotten.

I have seen the baths sparsely-populated at times, but never so utterly deserted as they were that Tuesday morning. The steam was far thicker than I had ever known it, and we proceeded with caution, for although Holmes voiced no concerns, I had no doubt he was as troubled as I was at the possibility that we might be walking into a trap.

'I was beginning to think you weren't coming,' a voice drawled out of the mist. 'That's quite far enough, if you don't mind. Well, well. The great Sherlock Holmes and his faithful biographer, I presume.'

I peered in the direction from which the address originated, but I could make out nothing beyond a vague shape obscured by steam.

'Holmes is my name, sir,' my friend replied. 'The adjective is your own. I take it you wish your identity to remain unknown to us.'

'A stunning display of ratiocination, Mr Holmes. Yes, I would prefer to avoid identification.'

'You are in danger, perhaps?' I suggested, finding a seat

with some difficulty.

'Not in the way you mean, Dr Watson. But the nature of my profession makes it vital that my name is kept out of the affair.'

'You have yet to tell us what that affair is,' Holmes said.

'Go to the home of Mr Alistair Sebastian, Mr Holmes. The Larches, Ham Common. There's something… provocative lodged in the chimney. A dead body.'

'How do you know this?' Holmes asked.

'Because I saw it, Mr Holmes.'

'Indeed? Your accent is against your being a chimney-sweep, still less a burglar.'

'Nevertheless, a burglar I am. Actually, I prefer the term "cracksman", but you understand my desire for anonymity. The chimney is quite a decent size. It struck me as a suitably original way of making an entrance. And with the festive season approaching, it seemed somehow appropriate.'

'And the body,' I asked, 'was it that of Alistair Sebastian?'

'I'm sure I couldn't say. The gloom, you know. One panics.'

'Perhaps,' suggested Holmes, 'your accomplice is not as familiar with Mr Sebastian as you are.'

'Now who says I have an accomplice?'

'Even the widest chimney could only provide sufficient space for an individual of slender form. I cannot make out your features clearly in this steam, but you appear to be of a more… athletic build.'

'My, my, your eyesight is as cultivated as your mind, it seems. Very well, it was my *accomplice* who discovered the body, not I. The original plan was that I was to lower him down the chimney, then he would unlock the front door and I would enter in a rather more mundane fashion. When Bu- *my accomplice* discovered the corpse, he went all to pieces and I was obliged to pull him up again.'

'Why are you telling us all this?' Holmes asked. 'Surely

you have nothing to gain by doing so.'

He did not reply immediately. 'Did you miss the part where I told you there was a dead man stuck up the chimney? He didn't climb up there looking for a place to nap. Clearly, someone put him there. Having inadvertently discovered him, I feel I have a certain responsibility to find out who killed him. And that responsibility I now pass on to you, Mr Holmes. I am nothing if not a good sport.'

'You have overlooked an item of importance. My fee.'

The man sighed. 'I supposed that the work might be its own reward – it is in my case – but one has to make a living, of course. Very well, Mr Holmes, you'll be suitably recompensed for your time and trouble.'

'You miss the point, sir. I have no wish to receive monies obtained illegally.'

'I once had a legitimate profession, but a Scots police inspector by the name of Mackenzie forced me to resign my post. Well-gotten gains are not so easy to come by these days.'

'Perhaps we can come to some arrangement. Provided, of course, that your claim is genuine. How am I to report my findings?'

'Today is Tuesday. Meet me here on Thursday at the same time.'

'And if I have no news to report?' Holmes asked. But he did not receive an answer. Our client had vanished.

The state of affairs with which we had been presented was more than slightly out of the ordinary, but as is well known, only the extraordinary was of interest to Sherlock Holmes. There now remained the question of whether the story we had been told at the Olympia was authentic, or simply an elaborate hoax.

Our first sight of the ill-omened house on Ham Common eliminated any doubt in my mind. A familiar figure clad in a disreputable raincoat and shabby black bowler gaped at us from the doorway.

'Mr Holmes!' gasped Inspector Lestrade. 'But how on earth… I only just sent the constable to the telegraph office.'

'We have other sources of information,' my friend replied, coolly. 'May we come in?'

The first sight that greeted our eyes upon entering the dining room was the body of a man slumped in a chair situated between a long polished table and the door. He was almost bald, save for a few thin strands of white hair, and the expression of horror on his moon-shaped face was one with which I was familiar. I was accustomed to seeing such ghastly constriction in cases of severe heart failure, but this was somehow different. I realised with growing unease that I might for the first time be looking at the features of a man who had been genuinely overcome by terror in the last moments of his life.

'Mind your feet, gentlemen, there's crushed glass all over the place,' Lestrade advised us. The Inspector's tone was conciliatory, his self-esteem having been badly dented by the affair of the Norwood Builder, some years before. 'Let me introduce you to the late Mr Alistair Sebastian, schoolteacher at St Ethelbert's, and owner of this house. *Former* owner.'

'Rather a grand residence for a schoolteacher,' I observed. Even at the height of my medical career, I would have been unable to afford such a sizeable home.

'He didn't turn up for lessons today, and he'd taken the previous afternoon off to see his doctor. A colleague came 'round to see if he was feeling alright. He got no answer at the front door, and when he looked in through the window, he saw… this.'

Holmes bent low over the body of Alistair Sebastian, gently examining the folds of his light-coloured clothing. There was no sign of any of the detritus one would expect to find on a body lodged in a chimney, nor did his size make such a position tenable. If Sebastian had been discovered in the chair, might there be a *second* body? My eyes drifted towards the large marble fireplace at the other end of the room.

'I must confess, gentlemen, I still can't be sure whether we're looking at a murder or not.' Lestrade's words wrested me from my grim imaginings. 'No signs of violence on the victim. Not that that means anything – you both recall the Lauriston Gardens business, I'm sure. And not even so much as a puncture mark on him. Not anywhere obvious, anyway. But there was someone else here last night; the two wineglasses attest to that. You don't think the wine could have been poisoned, do you, Mr Holmes?'

'At this stage it would be unwise to rule anything out,' Holmes replied. 'Mr Sebastian lived alone?'

'Except for two servants, a married couple off visiting a sick relative in Cricklewood. According to the neighbour, he was often visited by a brother, Edgar - some kind of auditor for the Government. There's another brother, Luther, younger than the other two. Not certain of his profession, or even if he has one, but apparently, *he* lives somewhere in the Ham Common area too, though he never comes 'round. Bad feeling between them, so says this neighbour. There's something else of interest.' Lestrade strode over to the fireplace that had already attracted my notice. 'You observe that there's a large amount of soot around here? Do you think it has any bearing on the case?'

'I'm afraid it means there's a body in the chimney, Inspector,' Holmes responded, levelly.

It was only with the assistance of the luckless Constable Woods, once he had returned from the telegraph office, that we were able to retrieve the body trapped in the flue. Once we had all four brushed as much coal-dust as possible from our attire, Holmes set about cleaning the dead man's face with a damp handkerchief. Even in the ghastliness of an agonising death, the family resemblance between the two men was obvious. This fellow was slimmer than Alistair, and as far as I could tell, there appeared to be little discernible age difference between them, save that the corpse in the chimney boasted a fuller head of hair. But were we looking at the body of Edgar or Luther Sebastian?

Lestrade shook his head in amazement. 'You never cease to astound me, Mr Holmes. I would never have imagined there might be another body up there.'

'I have my methods, Inspector.'

Yet again, there were no overt signs of violence to the body, save for the tearing of his clothes at the elbows and knees, no doubt suffered during a frantic scramble up the chimney. But a scramble from what or whom could not be determined, even after Holmes went over every inch of the room with his convex lens. His search concluded at the seated body of Alistair Sebastian. Extracting an envelope from his pocket, Holmes dropped to the floor and began collecting up all the pieces of broken glass.

'If you have no objections, Inspector,' said he, 'I will take these fragments back to Baker Street and examine them under my microscope. Perhaps we can meet there later and discuss any developments over supper and a cobwebby bottle.'

The policeman offered no objection, knowing full well that Holmes' scientific equipment was far superior to anything possessed by Scotland Yard.

The day had been a long one, but it was still only late-afternoon when we returned to our bachelor lodgings. Holmes set to work in gloomy silence at his chemical table, while I settled down with an unread copy of *The Lancet*. Eventually, it became clear that he would be about his labours for some hours to come. Knowing that my continued presence could serve no useful purpose, I decided to leave him to his labours, and spend the remainder of the day at my club.

Upon my return, Holmes was at last inclined to discuss his findings.

'Of course, we will have to wait for the results of Dr Litefoot's post-mortem, but I do not think I am too far out on a limb when I suggest that death was caused by asphyxiation after both men came into contact with a vial containing poison gas.'

'How came Edgar Sebastian's body in the chimney?' I asked.

'The gas was lighter than air. He could not escape it by the door, for his late brother barred the way. The windows are on the far side of the room – he could not reach them before the gas overtook him; the chimney was the only other option.'

'But the gas rose up it faster than he could climb.' said I.

'Either that, or he had sufficient on his clothing to incapacitate him before he got too far.'

'And you deduce all this from the examination of these fragments? How is it that you did not find the stopper used to prevent the gas escaping from the vial? We can hardly suggest that the killer took it with him, and somehow avoided being killed by his own weapon.'

'Indeed, how did he deliver the vial and make his escape?' Holmes added. 'Those matters remain unanswered. But the stopper could not be found because it did not exist.' Gingerly, he held up one of the larger pieces of glass he had recovered. 'I fancy this may have been the top of the vial. You see that it has been melted shut.'

'But why?'

'The contents would be in a partial vacuum, and the glass would break more easily. The gas would then explode out, covering a wide area.'

'Hideous!'

'But ingenious. We are dealing with a cunning mind, Watson. I fear that we are only scratching the surface of this case.'

Just then, Lestrade arrived, his face flushed with victory, his manner grossly triumphant, as I had not seen it in many a year.

'Well, there's still much that remains unclear,' he said, settling himself into a chair and helping himself to some cold cuts of meat, 'but I at least have our culprit under lock and key. His name is Luther Sebastian.'

'The other brother from Ham Common,' I said. 'Then the body in the chimney must have been Edgar.'

Lestrade produced from his overcoat pocket a framed photograph, which he handed to Holmes, who in turn passed it to me. The picture was of three men, two standing and one seated. I recognised the one on the left as Alistair Sebastian, whom we had discovered slumped in his chair earlier that same day. The fellow stood shoulder to shoulder with him was clearly Edgar Sebastian. When I had seen him last, he had been covered from head to toe in soot, but I now saw that his hair had been as black in life as it was in death. Both men wore deeply serious expressions, and I wondered whether their apparent disapproval might have been aimed at the third man in the picture. Luther Sebastian was at least ten years younger than his brothers, leaner, with a pencil thin moustache and features that seemed incapable of solemnity.

'All three brothers came into money six months ago,' Lestrade told us. 'Their uncle, who struck it rich in the Australian gold-fields, left them his entire fortune. I didn't have to make too many enquiries to discover that Luther has already gone through a sizeable portion of his share.'

'And thus found murder less burdensome than frugality. Is that your theory, Lestrade?' Holmes asked.

'If you mean he killed his brothers for their inheritances – yes, Mr Holmes, I believe he did.'

'Certainly a compelling motive,' I observed. 'Does he give an account of his whereabouts at the time of the murder, whenever that might have been?'

The inspector glanced at his notes again. 'Still waiting for an estimate from Dr Litefoot, but certainly later than half past four. After visiting his doctor - fellow named Makepeace, on Harley Street - Alistair caught the train home and arrived about quarter past four, a quarter of an hour before Edgar. Again, we have the neighbour to thank for that, nosey blighter.'

I wondered whether Alistair's doctor might be Gideon Makepeace. We belonged to the same club, and I had in fact seen him earlier that evening. I made a mental note to speak to him about the matter when next we met, not that there appeared to be any significance to it.

'At six that evening, Luther was busy being blackballed by the Bagatelle Club for non-payment of gambling debts. He says that after that, he wandered from tavern to tavern, but is unable to be more specific. He certainly reeked of alcohol when I nabbed him, but I've seen that trick before.'

Holmes remained silent for a full minute, his long, thin fingers steepled together as he considered this new information. Lestrade and I both knew better than to break his concentration.

'You said there was some bad feeling between Luther and Alistair?' he said at last.

'Between Luther and *both* his brothers. They thought he was more than a bit of a wastrel.'

'Then how did he gain entrance to the house? It is unthinkable that he had his own key and unlikely that either Alistair or Edgar might have let him in.'

Lestrade looked puzzled for a moment, before inspiration struck. 'I'll search his house! What's the betting I'll find a stolen or duplicate key - or a set of lockpicks! Then all that remains is to discover where and how he came by this poison gas.'

I had observed that something about this matter still troubled Holmes. Although he would not admit to as base an emotion as pride, I observed that it was not until after Lestrade's departure that he felt able to reveal the cause of his anxiety. 'I am out of my element, Watson. My scientific expertise does not extend into this region.'

'Then what are we to do?'

'There is a highly secret government establishment in Aldershot where experiments involving such gases are currently being undertaken. I think our wisest course is to consult the experts.'

'If it is so secret, may I ask how *you* know about it?'

Holmes smiled a thin smile. 'It is not for nothing that I am my brother's brother,' he said.

When we arrived at the laboratory in Aldershot – an unprepossessing red-brick building resembling a child's building block of great size – we experienced no difficulty in gaining entrance. No questions were raised at Holmes' use of his brother's name. He had once told me that, on occasion, Mycroft Holmes *was* the British Government, and the speed with which we found ourselves at the heart of that establishment showed that his claim was no idle boast. We were advised that the director would be notified of our presence, and asked to wait in his office. I have seen many similar governmental workplaces during my association with Sherlock Holmes, but there was something unusual about this one. At first, I was unable to account for my disquiet, but after a few minutes I realised that an acrid but not unfamiliar odour was assailing my nostrils.

'Holmes, that ghastly smell… I seem to know it from somewhere. What is it?'

'It is Green Tea,' two voices replied simultaneously. I turned to face the new arrival, and to my utter astonishment found myself looking into the onyx pupils of the very last person I expected to see - Professor Chen Takai.

After the Chinese poisoner's dramatic escape from police custody two years before, Holmes had been of the opinion that Chen had returned to his native land. But now here he was, clad not in a multi-coloured gown but in the drab clothing of the British civil servant, his once-long moustache trimmed to a less ostentatious length. He had lost weight, but even so, the swell of his stomach protested at the constraints of his Western garb.

I tried to speak, but found my vocal chords paralysed. Holmes had once voiced the opinion that Chen was an exponent of mesmerism, and indeed it would have been all too easy to lose oneself in those ebony pools that passed for eyes. It was not the force of his personality that silenced me, however, but rather shock and total disbelief. Holmes appeared equally stunned by the reappearance of his former antagonist.

'Please make yourselves comfortable, gentlemen,' said Chen, motioning toward a couple of chairs, as he took his place behind a desk. 'In the last two years, I have learned to accommodate some of your race's peculiarities, including your preference for chairs over cushions. My English, also, has improved more than somewhat, would you not say?'

'More than somewhat,' Holmes replied, coldly. He did not make a move toward the chairs, nor did I. 'You must excuse my momentary surprise, Professor. I had imagined that you were safely back in China.'

'Not an attractive consideration, Mr Holmes. I regret to say I have made my homeland...' he considered the appropriate phrase, 'too hot to hold me. Instead, I have accepted a post of some honour in this country. I have become, as you see, a Government Mandarin.'

'What might Scotland Yard might say if they were to

discover you here,' I wondered aloud.

Chen gave a childish and quite uncharacteristic grin in return. 'I think they would say very little, Dr Watson. You see, I am in a most exalted position.'

'No position is above the law,' I countered.

'You are wrong. I... walk between the raindrops. I have complete protection from prosecution for my former wrongdoings.'

'And your *present* wrongdoings?' Holmes asked.

Chen shook his head, as though he completely failed to understand the meaning of my friend's words. Having been so utterly humiliated by Holmes during their last encounter– which resulted in the poisoner being handcuffed to Inspector Lestrade and transported to Scotland Yard – he clearly relished the opportunity to toy with us now.

'The aim of your experiments is to discover a poison gas that will deliquesce when exposed to the air?' Holmes asked.

'Perhaps,' he said, coyly. Then, apparently realising that the only way to prolong our discomfort was to give out more information, he continued: 'A variant upon Hydrocyanic acid. Your English scientists were struggling because of its flammability and its tendency to condense in cold surroundings. Germany can be quite cold, you see.'

'So you volunteered your knowledge of chemicals unknown to European science.'

'I did not volunteer my knowledge, Mr Holmes; it was sought. This work is my penance. As you know, I have a history of misdeeds.'

'If I may say so,' I observed, 'you do not appear to be in too much discomfort.'

'You mock me, Dr Watson, but when war comes I shall be looked upon as a hero.'

'You are a common murderer.'

'I am an exceptional murderer.'

'And you continue to ply your original trade,' Holmes growled. 'You provided Luther Sebastian with a poison gas which he used to dispose of his wealthy brothers.'

The accusation was not without merit. It had been with the use of a vial of a different gas concealed in his sleeve that Chen had been able to incapacitate Lestrade and escape from custody years before.

Again, the Chinaman shook his head. I was reminded of Holmes' original assessment of our foe – *The man emits evil like an odour. Too long in his company and one might find it suffocating.*

'I know of no-one named Luther Sebastian,' Chen said.

'You cannot expect me to believe that. You are a killer by nature as well as by profession. That weakness will be your undoing.'

Chen pretended to straighten some papers on his desk before speaking again. 'I have no siblings, but it seems to me that they are a cause of considerable – is "strife" the correct word? For instance, you claim that this Luther Sebastian is responsible for the murder of his brothers. And you, Mr Holmes, wish to see me on the gallows, whereas it is *your* brother I have to thank for my current situation.'

Where Holmes had been unable to disguise his shock at Chen's unexpected appearance, he now masked his incredulity quite effectively. Nevertheless, I observed the muscles in his neck tightening.

There was no way to depart from that interview with a sense of dignity. It was obvious that any attempt to remove Chen from his place of work would meet with failure, and Holmes was reduced to issuing a few warnings of dire consequences – all of which failed to make an impact upon their target – before marching out. I followed, feeling confused, frustrated and impotent.

Holmes would not speak during our carriage journey to

Whitehall, and I refrained from attempting to draw him out; his knitted brows and abstracted air spoke of his present preoccupation more loudly than words could.

It had been several years since I had seen Mycroft Holmes last, but I was astonished to discover that his weight had increased considerably. My surprise was all the greater for the fact that, on our two previous encounters, his extraordinary corpulence was the first thing to catch the eye. The indolence suggested by his frame was, however, at odds with his features – a masterful brow, steel-gray, deep-set eyes that seemed to always retain that far-away, introspective look which I had only observed in Sherlock's when he was exerting his full powers.

His office was a far from grand affair, no larger than Chen's with a row of filing cabinets covering one wall and an improbably large globe the only concession to individuality. Twin bookcases faced one another across the room, one weighed down with volumes relating to finance, the other devoted to international politics. It was far from what I expected for the domain of one who possessed such influence.

'My, my, two visits in one year,' said Mycroft, jovially, as he poured wine into three waiting glasses. 'Mother would be thrilled that we are seeing so much of one another these days. Isn't it ridiculous? Two brothers, living in the same city…'

'The same city but different worlds,' responded Holmes.

Mycroft completed his task at last, and raised his own glass as though about to propose a toast. 'Let us celebrate the occasion by finishing off this excellent Madeira. 1814 - one year before Waterloo, you know.'

'Such generosity!' Holmes exclaimed. 'For one so famously unclubbable, it must come as a shock to learn that news of your hospitality has reached China.'

The glass in Mycroft's hand stopped an inch from his lips. 'Ah,' he breathed. '*That*. Very well, how much do you know, or *think* you know?'

'I know that the British Government is employing a murderer in their laboratories at Aldershot.'

Mycroft replaced his wineglass. 'The British Government is doing nothing of the sort. The charge against Chen Ta-kai was, I understand, *Attempted* Murder.'

'A convenient but meaningless distinction. You know as well as I that he has been implicated in a dozen poisonings.'

'*Implicated*, my dear brother. Another important distinction. Your scruples do you credit, Sherlock, but a man in my position cannot afford such luxuries. There are certain affairs that do not come within the province of the consulting detective; they have to be dealt with on an altogether different level.'

'And does that include the development of poison gases at a laboratory based in Aldershot?'

'Its existence is a closely-guarded secret. How did you come to know of it?'

'You told me.'

'I most certainly did nothing of the kind! As I recall, you once asked me whether such an establishment existed and I denied the fact.'

'True, but as you did so, I observed a slight ripple in your snifter of brandy.'

Mycroft murmured something unintelligible, as though cursing his perceived indiscretion. Under his brother's steely gaze, he merely shrugged, and said in justification of his actions, '*Inter arma enim silent leges*.'

I felt duty bound to point out to Mr Holmes that we were not presently at war.

'But war is inevitable, Doctor. Our experts, of whom I am naturally the foremost, are convinced of that. If we are to have any advantage, we must investigate the opportunities offered by chemical weaponry. Ibbetson, our man in Friedrichshafen, has supplied documents indicating that the Kaiser has sanctioned a similar undertaking.'

'And to that end, you have enlisted one of the most dangerous men alive to assist you,' Holmes snapped.

'One of the most brilliant men alive also. Professor Chen's work is decades ahead of its time. There's no-one on our side capable of duplicating it.'

'It may interest you to know that Chen's "work" is responsible for the deaths of two men.'

Mycroft remained impassive.

'Of course,' Holmes went on, 'how foolish of me. You know that already. I doubt that nothing of importance goes on in any branch of the official services that you are not made aware of within minutes.'

'Perhaps a little longer than that, Sherlock, but I cannot deny it. There is no doubt that the deaths of Edgar and Alistair Sebastian tally with Chen's researches, but I do not see that any reason exists to link him to the crime.'

'Save the fact that those researches are decades ahead of their time, with no-one capable of duplicating them.'

'That we know of. I understand that your trained bloodhound, Inspector Lestrade, has made out a strong case against the surviving brother, *Luther* Sebastian.'

'Do you truly believe that a young idler is capable of succeeding where your best scientists have failed? The arm of coincidence is long, but not so long as that, surely. The Professor is playing you for a fool, Mycroft, simply because he can. He sees no reason to bring a halt to his criminal career; in fact, your patronage only makes it easier for him to act with impunity.'

For the first time during our interview, I detected signs of unease in the elder Holmes' features. Then he flashed a mirthless smile at me. 'My brother seems to have quite a resentment of professors, don't you think, Doctor? I wonder if it relates back to his intense dislike of our mathematics tutor. Very well, Sherlock. If you can present me with evidence of a connection between Chen and Luther Sebastian, that would be a different matter. My advice to you is to seek it out, if it exists.' He glanced at his watch. 'It is now a quarter past five and I am fully a half-hour late for the Diogenes Club. I'm afraid I must terminate this interview forthwith, or risk causing widespread panic among the staff. Good-day to you, Sherlock, Doctor.'

'You have made a bargain with the Devil, brother,' Holmes almost whispered. 'God help you.'

Mycroft was unaffected. 'If Germany develops these weapons before England, God help us all.'

Holmes remained in sombre mood for the remainder of the day. Again, I said nothing, for fear of placing an already painful situation into sharp relief. I knew that he felt his brother's betrayal as keenly as if he had been run through with a rapier.

Upon our return to Baker Street, he constructed a small mound of cushions and placed a selection of pipes on the floor before him. Clearly, he intended to spend the evening introspecting. Having drained every last drop of information from the latest copy of *The Lancet*, I concluded that nothing could be gained from my continued presence, and though the atmosphere in our rooms would be less poisonous than in Alistair Sebastian's home, I did not relish the prospect of enduring it for the remainder of the night.

It was gone eleven when I returned to Baker Street. Holmes had consumed every last ounce of tobacco, and though still awake, made no attempt to respond to my queries regarding the case.

'Oh, by the way,' I said as a last resort, 'you recall I told

93

you that I know Alistair Sebastian's doctor, Gideon Makepeace? Well, I bumped into him at the club tonight.' Holmes raised an eyebrow. 'Indeed?'

'I didn't discover anything of interest, I'm afraid. The patient had been complaining of numbness in his hands and fingers. Makepeace diagnosed it as Rheumatoid Arthritis. Hereditary complaint, apparently. It killed his father.'

For the first time since we had begun this singular investigation, could I observe that sudden brightening of his eyes and tightening of his lips, which told me that at last Holmes saw some gleam of light in this utter darkness.

'I think the same may well have been true for Alistair,' he said in reply.

To my shame, I must confess that the next morning I had quite forgotten we were due to meet once more with our mysterious client. Holmes' sole contribution to our cab journey to the Olympia Baths was to ask that I accompany him to Mycroft's office the next day.

'It is really quite ridiculous, but I always seem to be overawed by Mycroft. I'd be grateful for your presence, old fellow. I never quite know what to say to him when we're alone.'

A further surprise awaited us at the Olympia – the honourable cracksman was nowhere to be found.

'I suppose he could have been arrested in the interim,' I suggested.

'I hardly think so,' said a familiar voice. I turned this way and that, expecting to see a vague form in the steam. But this time, I saw no-one.

'Where are you?' I demanded. 'What's the matter with your voice?'

'He's speaking to us through the ventilator,' Holmes

explained. 'Fool! I should have anticipated it.'

'We all have our off-days, Mr Holmes. I had mine on board the steamship *Uhlan*. 'Incidentally, I must request that you don't attempt to track me down. I should view that as the most shameful betrayal of our relationship.'

'I would not dream of it, I assure you, sir,' my friend replied.

'I shall take you at your word, then. Now, what have you to report?'

'The case is solved.'

Holmes' announcement was the first indication of this I had received. I believe I stared at Holmes in astonishment, but given the thickness of the steam, my actions were quite useless.

'I am delighted to hear it,' said the cracksman. 'Please don't waste your time boring me with the details; I look forward to reading about it in the crime news. Well, it appears our business is at an end.'

'Not quite, sir. There are some quite weighty problems still to be resolved, one of them the small matter of my fee.'

From the ventilator came a weary sigh.

'And since I do not feel that I can accept money or valuables, I shall have to request payment in kind.'

Sherlock Holmes was silent as emptied a packet of papers on to his brother's desk. The elder Holmes examined them for some minutes. At last, he said, 'Well, obviously this changes matters.'

'Does it?' asked the detective. 'I confess that I was somewhat slow in making the connection, but I have always held that you have the greater intellect, Brother. No doubt you had already deduced that Chen supplied the gas sample not to Luther but to *Edgar* Sebastian.'

'You pay me too much credit, Sherlock.'

'Edgar's role of Government auditor no doubt provided him with sufficient information concerning the goings-on at Aldershot and the appointment of the notorious Professor Chen Ta-kai.'

Realisation dawned upon me. 'Then it was Alistair and Edgar who were looking for a way of disposing of Luther, and not the other way around.'

Holmes nodded. 'I fear that enforced retirement cannot be far off if I continue to make such obvious errors. I failed to observe one of my own maxims, namely that there is nothing more deceptive than an obvious fact. For half a year, the elder brothers watched the profligate Luther fritter away his third of the family fortune. Surely it would be better if the money were in their pockets instead. They had to stop him before it was all gone. Chen provided Edgar with the means for, I imagine, a not-inconsiderable fee. Edgar passed the vial of poison gas to Alistair, with the notion that he would then unleash it on Luther, another resident of the Ham Common area. How he planned to do it, we can only surmise. Perhaps dropped through an open window, or the letterbox or… the chimney. In any case, their plans went awry quite dramatically. Alistair, it appears, was in the early stages of arthritis. When Edgar handed him the vial, his fingers could not grasp it, and to their shared horror, it fell to the floor and smashed, releasing its deadly contents. Alistair died instantly, while Edgar tried to escape, but- well, you knew what had occurred before I did. I will always wonder precisely how much you *did* know and when you knew it. Had I not presented you with these proofs of meetings between Edgar and Chen, I believe you would have allowed Chen to go on working at Aldershot.'

'All men have their beliefs, Sherlock. I am quite as devoted to mine as you are to yours, and I hold your abilities in higher esteem than you realise. I anticipated an outcome of this sort. As we speak, Chen is on his way back to his native land. I understand that the Chinese authorities are anxious to speak to him about several murders, the reason he left in the first place. I imagine that makes you very happy.'

'Hardly. There remains the matter of his work at Aldershot.'

Mycroft studied both his brother's expression and then mine before focussing on Sherlock once more.

'There was a break-in at the laboratory last night. Chen's notes were taken, and as I have commented, no scientist in England is capable of duplicating his work. I suppose I have you to thank for that, Sherlock?'

'My own skills at housebreaking are not inconsiderable, but I am not so adept that I could penetrate the security of a secret Government establishment. I fear you will have to look elsewhere for your culprit, although I have no doubt he has destroyed the Professor's research. All that intrigue for naught.'

However I was expecting Mycroft to react at that moment, his response took me completely off-guard.

'Can I expect you 'round for tea on Saturday, Sherlock?'

THE ADVENTURE OF THE HANGING TYRANT

1. A LETTER FROM A CLIENT

I believe I can say with all honesty that, following a period of several years during which he was believed dead by all but two people, nowhere was the surprise and disbelief resulting from the return of Mr Sherlock Holmes to public life felt more powerfully than in my own household. After the death of my beloved wife, I had dedicated my life and, save for a few hours a week spent at my club, all of my time to my medical practice. To the extent that any man who has lost that which made his life meaningful can be said to be happy, I believe I can claim that I was happy. Or, at the very least, I was not unhappy, which doubtless amounts to the same thing.

But in the spring of the year 1894, I was astonished to discover that my friend Sherlock Holmes was not dead, but alive and well and standing before me in the study of my Kensington home, having evaded the clutches of his arch-nemesis, the late Professor Moriarty. Now, some months later, I stood alone in that same study contemplating the wallpaper for which I had never truly cared but had voiced no objection to when my dear wife Mary had selected it. 'The bright colours will cheer your patients, James,' she had said. In truth, there was nothing else left in the room to contemplate, all of my possessions being stored currently in the furniture van waiting at my front door. I am no longer certain exactly how I reached my decision, but I had chosen to throw in my lot with Holmes once more and return to the Baker Street address which had been my home for many years during my bachelor days. Was I mad to hope that I would again be swept up in the hectic adventures that had been such an essential part of my existence for the best part of a decade? To my knowledge, Holmes had already turned down one potential and influential client just a few weeks earlier. I was by no means completely comfortable with this change of direction in my life, but I made it simply for the sake of doing *something*. I might just as easily have boarded a vessel bound for Australia or attempted to rejoin my old regiment. Holmes' reappearance in my life had filled me not with a sense of relief but one of total confusion. My wife was dead and my best friend, whom I had believed dead, was alive. The situation was the cause of many contradictory emotions, none of which I would have dreamed of burdening Holmes with and none of which, I am pleased to say, I can recall accurately today.

A fist rapped politely on the open door behind me.

'I shan't be much longer,' said I, over my shoulder. 'I am almost ready to go.'

'I am delighted to hear you say so,' a well-known voice replied. 'There is not a moment to be lost, Watson. We are expected in Pangbourne by noon. If we hurry, we can just make the next train from Paddington.'

I turned to discover Sherlock Holmes waiting in the doorway, clad in his long grey travelling coat, and effecting what I might almost describe as a warm smile.

'Holmes!' I cried. And then, after I had taken in his last remark: 'To Pangbourne, now? But what about my furniture?'

'It will, I am certain, be waiting for you at Baker Street upon our return. Your hat and boots, old friend, and don't dilly-dally!'

We were barely in time for the Berkshire-bound train and we had only just settled down in our carriage before I began to feel overcome by weariness. I had experienced an unaccountably restless night and I intended to shut my eyes for only a short time. How much of our journey had elapsed before I was suddenly snapped back to wakefulness by Holmes' abrupt tone I could not say.

'Watson! I said, there might be some danger involved. I trust that you are carrying your service revolver?'

'Sorry, Holmes,' said I, attempting to stifle a yawn with the back of my hand. 'It is presently on its way to Baker Street with the rest of my possessions. I had no idea we would be drawn into a case so soon.'

'Ah, well, it may be that our correspondent overestimates the threat against her.'

'Threat? Holmes, you seem to be developing an appalling habit of starting a story from the middle. You forget that I have no knowledge of any of this.'

Without replying, Holmes extracted a folded sheet of writing paper from his jacket pocket and held it out to me. 'From your- from *our* client?'

'A most provocative letter, Watson. Kindly refresh my memory as to its contents.'

Holmes' remarkable faculty for storing the smallest details (despite his claims to the contrary) made this exercise entirely unnecessary, but he always seemed to derive some satisfaction from hearing his correspondence read aloud, so I obliged gladly. The letter was addressed 'Field House, Pangbourne' and ran thus:

'DEAR MR HOLMES – I have recently had a most troubling experience and am uncertain to whom I should turn for advice and assistance. The newspapers have been full of your astonishing return from the dead, and I am all too aware from your good friend Dr Watson's stories that you are possessed of both great intelligence and great wisdom.'

'My blushes, Watson!' Holmes interrupted.

The letter went on:

'Please forgive my reticence in providing details and my unwillingness to call upon you in London. If there is any danger to be faced, I should not wish the servants to confront it on my behalf.

'I should be most grateful if you would call upon me at

noon tomorrow. Please arrange for Dr Watson to accompany you. I cannot guarantee that you will be granted admittance in his absence.

'Yours faithfully

'MRS FRANCIS CARTNER'

I found the content of the letter intriguing, not least because my presence seemed so important to the writer. Was she unwell, perhaps, and in need of the services of a doctor? I put the matter to Holmes.

'It is certainly very puzzling,' he replied, 'and we cannot know the answer until we have spoken to our client. Yes, I have decided to accept her case even though doing so breaks the rule I enforced with such fierceness only a fortnight ago. However, the matter is simply too intriguing and the lady is clearly in need of my - what was it? -great intelligence and great wisdom. We can, at any rate, form a few conclusions about her circumstances and personality from her letter. She is clearly a woman of strong character, and she was once quite wealthy, but has had to make some quite severe adjustments to her lifestyle, no doubt following the death of her husband. How unfortunate to be both widowed *and* childless.'

'And to think that a while ago you were concerned that your abilities were failing you! The writer's strong character I can see from the content of her letter, but as for her failing fortunes, I confess I did not read anything that indicated such a condition. She writes that she keeps servants.'

'Until recently, Watson, you had servants also, and very attentive servants at that.'

I had no idea how Holmes reached such a conclusion. I had found Megan even more insolent and lazy than Mary Jane Kelly, and I had been only too pleased to give her notice.

'My reasoning is based upon the letter itself, not its subject matter. The paper is of the very best quality, but there is a tear on the left side, just below the crease. That tear did not occur after writing, for the lady has taken pains to avoid it; the line beginning "great wisdom" is deliberately out of true. Now, why should an affluent writer not simply use a sheet that is not torn? On its own, this is merely suggestive, but observe that the ink, again of the finest sort, has run out early in the final paragraph. The replacement ink is of a cheap variety, common to most hotels. You will recall that during the von Lammerain blackmail case, I made a special study of the history and manufacture of ink. I have not yet written a monograph upon the subject, but I intend to do so when time permits. The combination of factors can lead only to the conclusion that our correspondent is using her final sheet of expensive paper and her final bottle of expensive ink to summon us. We should feel flattered therefore.'

'That is perfectly sound reasoning,' I confessed, 'but I do not see how you can tell that the lady is widowed. She signs herself "Mrs Cartner", after all.'

'Then why does she not turn to her husband in this time of peril, Watson? Why write to us? Why does her husband not send her away and out of danger? It will not do.'

'He might be elsewhere – perhaps his business requires that he travel.'

'A fair objection, Watson, it is good to see that you are keeping up. But was there ever a husband who would allow his employment to keep him from his wife's side if he believed her in danger? Again I ask, where is the husband, if not dead?'

'Divorced!' I announced, triumphantly. 'The husband wants nothing more to do with her, and so she must face this burden, whatever it is, alone.'

'You paint a vivid picture, doctor. I might add, in favour of your objection, that a lady might continue to use her married name after her divorce. Congratulations, old friend. It appears that your sleep has done your intellectual capacities some good.'

I felt a keen pleasure at these complimentary words, such as I had not felt for many a year.

'Then you agree with my conclusions, Holmes?'

'Not in the slightest, you are wholly incorrect.'

'Oh.'

'But you have certainly grasped the method, to consider all probable explanations before determining the only possible conclusion. But you remain too timid in your inferences. If this woman is divorced as you suggest, surely she must have secured some sort of financial settlement from her former husband. Why is she now reduced to writing to complete strangers on torn paper with inferior ink?'

I slumped back in my seat, defeated. After nearly fifteen years of acquaintance, on and off, I ought to have learned not to question my friend's logic. But I suppose that I should never appreciate the wonder of his gifts were I to accept it all with no objection. His ingenious observations had, however, caused me some disappointment in my own abilities; I had wished to surprise Holmes with a display of deductive reason regarding the letter writer, but had been unable to contribute anything of worth. As I mulled this over, a thought sprang to mind.

'Wait, Holmes!' I said. 'You say that this woman is childless – I believe that I can see your reasoning in that she would surely send her children away rather than see them at risk, and that such a caring mother could not bear to be separated from her offspring.'

Holmes merely nodded in reply.

'But might not the writer be an elderly woman, whose children have grown up and left home? I know what you are about to say, that they would surely wish to protect their mother as any husband would his wife, but what if she had only daughters and no sons? Surely, she would not place them in a perilous situation.'

Holmes gave a slight groan, as though in some discomfort. 'It was my understanding, doctor, that you have attempted to keep up the good work during my time away from London, is that not so?'

'Largely for my private satisfaction, but in my own small way, yes,' I replied, modestly.

'Then it disappoints me to learn that you have not studied my writings on the science of detection. You recall the puzzle at Reigate?'

'The matter involving the local squire?'

'*Squires*, Watson. Your inability to recall such pertinent details no doubt explains your failure to recollect my familiarity with the study of handwriting. A woman's age can be ascertained as tolerably as a man's and this is a woman who, while no longer in the first flush of youth, is very far from the bath chair. There is passion in her *D*s and vigour in her *T*s. In the past three years I have extended my studies to include numerous languages and alphabets, and I believe that my monograph upon the subject is due for some revising. I may wish you to take notes when the time is propitious, Watson.'

And with that, he closed his eyes and remained motionless until our arrival. I attempted to return to my earlier slumber, but found myself completely unable to relax, wondering as I did whether the mystery that was about to be placed before us would afford me an opportunity to prove to Holmes that my skills had improved to such a degree over the last three years that I could claim without affectation to be his equal as a detective.

2. THE STRANGE STORY OF BASIL VALENTINE

From Sherlock Holmes' description of Mrs Cartner's failing resources, I had expected to find the lady residing in the sort of homely cottage that Mary and I had often discussed when planning my eventual retirement from medicine. Instead, we discovered Field House to be quite a large affair that, in former times would no doubt have been considered almost grand. As we alighted from our wagonette, it became clear that the building was in a poor state of repair. A climbing plant of some variety – now completely dead - covered much of the front of the house. I considered this, and was suddenly aware of a flurry of movement behind one of the windows.

'I observe it also, Watson,' said Holmes, before I had the opportunity to remark upon it. 'Be on your guard. I must confess, I am beginning to experience some apprehension about asking you to accompany me here.'

'And had I not, who knows what might have happened to you?' I replied as we made our way slowly to the front door, the pebbles crunching beneath our shoes with each step.

'You forget Watson, that I have already been dead. The experience is quite liberating.'

Holmes rapped on the door with a confidence I must confess I did not feel also. A moment later it opened a few inches, sufficient for me to observe the shape of a man blocking our entrance. I could ascertain no further details other than that he was of a stocky build and in height an inch or two shorter than I.

'Who are you gentlemen and what is the meaning of this call?' he growled.

'Not the welcome I was expecting, Watson,' the detective remarked, deliberately ignoring the menace implicit in the man's tone. Given the unpredictable nature of his own recent caller, I should have imagined that Holmes might have thought better of this off-hand approach.

From within the house, I heard a cultured female voice say: 'That will do, Peter. You are Sherlock Holmes?'

Holmes removed his travelling cap. 'I am, ma'am. My friend, Dr Watson.'

Unable to see the speaker, and feeling somewhat foolish, I

followed Holmes' lead in removing my hat. Clearly, we were being inspected, but for what purpose I could not imagine.

'You are not unlike your pictures, Mr Holmes.'

'So I am told, Mrs Cartner, but I fancy that greater justice has been done by the doctor's likeness than mine.'

'You have a moustache, doctor.'

I was somewhat nonplussed by this observation and, feeling more than a little foolish, I could think of no more profound reply than to agree that I did indeed have a moustache.

'I always wondered whether you actually would,' she said. Her voice was low and pleasing, but there was a strange quality to it; I wondered whether it might be fear. 'You are always pictured as wearing a moustache, but you have never referred to it in your stories.'

'I, er, believe that I may have mentioned it in *The Naval Treaty*, one of my later efforts.'

'Watson rarely places sufficient emphasis on his own excellent qualities,' Holmes offered. 'Mrs Cartner, I am only too happy to stand out here all day discussing the work of Mr Walter Paget-'

'Sidney,' I corrected.

'-Sidney, thank-you, Watson, but you summoned us both here for a more serious purpose, I imagine. May we be allowed to enter and discuss it at leisure?'

There was a moment's wait, during which, I supposed, the lady of the house must have indicated to her man, Peter, that we be allowed to pass him. It struck me as I entered that although it was early afternoon on a pleasant spring day outside the house, in the hallway it felt and appeared closer to early evening. An unmistakable musty odour reached my nostrils. As my eyes roamed the walls in search of traces of damp on the wallpaper, Peter, the formidable manservant, came into my view. His grizzled features and muscular frame could hardly have been considered a pleasant subject for close inspection at the best of times and it was clear that nothing I could say would budge the man if he did not wish to be budged. I craned my neck in an attempt to see our troubled letter writer positioned behind him. It must have been evident from my reaction that I was quite surprised by what I found.

'Are you unwell, Doctor Watson?' the lady asked.

I have heard many women on several continents described as 'handsome', but the phrase never seemed appropriate when – many years later – I was to compare them all to Mrs Francis Cartner. She was, I imagined, not quite forty, nearly as tall as I, dark-haired and blessed with a pleasing regularity of feature. The true individuality of her beauty, however, must surely have been her piercing blue eyes. I must admit that I was quite distracted by them, and a moment passed in silence before I realised that she had spoken to me.

'I am... quite well, Mrs Cartner. That is-'

'I fear that Watson is not a good traveller and our rather frantic journey here has quite unsettled his nerves,' Holmes interjected. I agreed that this might well be the case and Mrs Cartner insisted that I be allowed to sit and gather my wits. Taking our outer clothing with some apparent resentment, Peter led us into a sitting room made surprisingly cheerful by the bright sunlight beaming in from a large picture window. I noted the unusually grand and expensive items of furniture on display, quite at odds with the general state of the property. We were invited to sit and Peter was instructed to have the maid bring tea.

'By any chance, would it be possible to request coffee?' I asked, hesitantly. 'I know that it is not quite the time, but I have not had...'

A barely perceptible crease at each corner of her small but sensitive mouth was the only indication that I had embarrassed our host in some way.

'I am sorry to say that we have none, doctor, nor any strong liquor. In the last year, I have been forced to make some rather drastic economies.'

'It is really of no matter,' I assured her hurriedly. 'It was merely a whim.'

'Following the death of my husband,' she went on, seeming not to hear my last remark, 'I was horrified to learn that the solicitor responsible for managing his financial affairs, a Mr Ronald Sawyer, had misappropriated that income and – when the situation became known - absconded with much of it. My husband was the founder of the Haydock Tobacco Company, and had amassed a considerable sum in a very short time. When we married, he had already sold his interests in the firm and was content to live off his early profits for the remainder of his life. A life that was too prove all too short, gentlemen, for last February he succumbed to a family illness and it became clear that, although not poor, I had been robbed of much of the hard-earned money Francis would have wished me to have. I need hardly say that if I were asked to choose between wealth and having my husband restored to me, I should wish to have Francis always at my side.'

For a terrible moment, I recalled the wording of her letter and feared that Mrs Cartner was of the opinion that Holmes actually *had* returned from the dead and was on the brink of requesting that he retrieve her husband from the afterlife.

'But I am reconciled to the fact that I will not see him again, just as I am reconciled to the fact that the man who stole those funds will never be brought to justice. Mr Sawyer was last heard of in Ceylon, I have been informed. I am a realist and I sought thereafter to tailor my life to my ability to pay my way. I have been forced to sell what valuables I could bear to part with – a Greuze painting brought a very good price from a scholar who professed to being something of a collector.'

Holmes raised an inquisitive eyebrow.

'The final degradation for me came the day it became clear that I could no longer maintain our family home with its large staff. I gave notice to the majority of the servants, put the sale of the house in the hands of an agent more trustworthy than Mr Sawyer, and moved the remainder of my belongings – all that you see around you, gentlemen – into one of my husband's smaller properties, which he kept for letting purposes only, although I now know that what little profit arose from both houses did not go into my husband's account with Silvester's.' This brave speech was made without any discernible emotion on the part of the speaker. I was much impressed with the determination and strength of character she displayed in the face of such a devastating alteration to her circumstances, to say nothing of her commendable frankness.

'I hope that you will forgive the behaviour of my manservant, Peter, upon your arrival. He is fiercely protective of me and I believe that he would remain in my service even if I were unable to pay his wages, a day I fear may come sooner rather than later.'

Holmes leaned forward in his chair. 'And does Peter have good reason to be protective, madam? You state that you believe yourself in danger. From whom?'

'I… I have only seen one of them at close quarters,' she replied, with the first trace of hesitancy, 'the man who calls himself Basil Valentine.'

'Basil, did you say?' Holmes asked. 'The name is oddly familiar to me. But please relate to me the nature of your meeting with this Mr Valentine.'

Mrs Cartner folded her hands in her lap; a dignified act of self-composure, I thought. 'He wrote to me on the fifth. I regret to say that I did not retain the letter, which merely stated that the writer intended to call upon me with some information he believed would be to my advantage. Some odd presentiment, however, led me to put his business card in a safe place. It is on the table before you.'

'A model client, Holmes,' I noted.

'It is a great pity that the letter has been disposed of – it might have been quite instructive,' Holmes responded, somewhat grumpily. Without bothering to ask whether he might be permitted to examine it, he snatched up the card and scrutinised it. I wondered whether he might employ his high-powered lens upon the task, but he seemed not to find much that interested him in the card.

'There is little here that is of any use. The card reads: "Basil Valentine, Professor of Arcane Antiquities, University of Wittenberg", an institution renowned for its unconventional ex-students. I do not suppose that, if we were to make enquiries the University would ever have heard of a person purporting to hold such a vaguely defined position. Any scoundrel with an ounce of ingenuity could arrange for the printing of such a card. I have done so myself.'

I took the card from his fingers and studied it intently, hoping to spot some feature that my friend may have missed. 'Holmes, there is a thumb-mark on the reverse of this card,' I remarked

'Probably the printer's,' Holmes replied, without bothering to see my discovery for himself. 'I have yet to investigate a case in which the identification of such a mark has had any bearing on its solution.'

'I have done a great deal of reading on the subject over the last few years, and I understand that every fingerprint is unique and cannot be duplicated.'

'I have heard something of the kind; I remain unconvinced.'

Feeling somewhat embarrassed by his dismissal of this clue, I replaced the card on the table. Looking into our client's clear blue eyes, I gave her what I hoped would appear to be a smile of reassurance. I was glad to note that the gesture was returned.

Appearing not to notice, Holmes resumed his questioning. 'You permitted Mr Valentine to call?'

'His letter did not offer me the opportunity to give my permission or to withhold it, Mr Holmes; it simply stated that he would arrive the next day. Impertinent it undoubtedly was, but I imagined – foolishly, as I now realise – that he might know of a way in which my fortunes might somehow be improved. Not, of course, that money is the most important thing of which I have been deprived of late. If I had not been at such a low ebb at the time the letter arrived, I might well have refused. I wonder how differently events might have transpired if I had done so.'

The lady began to drift into a melancholy state once more. I could not, of course, blame her for that. More than once during that period in my life I had found myself descending into a deep funk without any apparent cause. I had learned that work was the best antidote to sorrow, but Mrs Cartner could not, of course, avail herself of that solution.

'Please relate the details of Mr Valentine's visit,' Holmes said, sharply, breaking our host out of her gloom. 'And try to include as much detail, however irrelevant you may consider it.' He leaned back in his seat and pressed his long fingers together, but – in deference to our client – his eyes remained open and keen.

'I have to say that I consider everything about the man to be irrelevant. When he arrived, one week ago tomorrow, it was apparent to me that he was scarcely the sort of gentleman who could have been a professor of any subject. I wondered whether he wore such a large moustache – your own, doctor, would be called modest by comparison – in order to hide his true appearance or his true age, for he could not have been older than twenty-five. To add to his improbable appearance, his taste in

111

clothes might, I imagine, have been better suited to a comedian of the music hall stage. The checks on his jacket were overstated to the point of vulgarity.'

I was reminded by this remark of our old friend Sir Henry Baskerville. 'Might he not,' I suggested, 'have been a Canadian or an American? Both nationalities' choice of attire is often less restrained than our own.'

She shook her head gently, a most captivating gesture. 'No, Dr Watson, I am certain that he was an Englishman. Unless, of course, he was an exceptional actor, and the improbability of his story makes me doubt that.'

'And what was that story?' Holmes prompted.

'He related it to me in this very room. I was seated in this same chair, but Mr Valentine could not be persuaded to sit. Instead he paced the floor, walking up to the window and back again several times. I did not think such agitation particularly strange, since by this point I had ascertained that there was nothing about the man that was not strange.

' "I suppose that the name Edward Kelley is unfamiliar to you, dear lady?" he asked.

' "I do not believe that I have ever met anyone of that name," I replied.

'He guffawed in a manner I considered more appropriate to the smoking room. "No indeed!" he barked. "It is not likely that you should, for he lived and died some centuries before you were born! Kelley, also known as Talbot, was the son of a humble baker, but he became one of England's greatest alchemists, and I know what you are thinking about *that*!"

'In truth, I doubted very much that Mr Valentine knew what I was thinking at that moment.

' "Alchemy, my dear lady, is commonly thought by an ignorant public to be the act of turning lead into gold, which any person with a jot of intelligence will tell you is impossible. In fact, alchemists, as the name suggests, experimented with all manner of chemicals for many purposes, the majority of them a good deal more practical than the accumulation of shiny metals. I think it is safe to say that we would have no doctors today were it not for the pioneering work of these alchemists – why, we might still be sticking leeches on one another!"

'I began to fear that my it was my visitor's intention to attempt to sell me something, and I pondered how best he might be ejected from Field House before the interview took a disagreeable turn.

' "Exactly two hundred and twenty one years ago, Kelley is believed to have been in this area and to have purchased, along with an alchemical tract entitled *The Book of St Dunstan*, a vial of red powder said to posses remarkable properties. Of course, in books and letters of the time, these properties were described as either magical in nature or else the power of the Almighty, but in these enlightened times one may see past the ignorance of a former age and understand this powder to be an extraordinary medicinal compound. Kelley buried the vial in an unknown location and no more of it is known to exist, but if it were ever to be unearthed, it could be analysed by one of our prominent scientists, and hopefully duplicated. It might prove invaluable in aiding patients to recover from surgical procedures. My own dear brother was injured so badly during the war in Afghanistan that his leg was amputated and the fellow died three days later from the shock. If the doctors had had access to Kelley's extraordinary red powder… well, dear John might still be with us today."

'I need hardly tell you gentleman that I believed not one word of this preposterous yarn, including the details of this unfortunate brother. I decided that it was time to get to the crux of the matter.

' "This might be a very pretty story to a collector of fairy tales, Mr Valentine," said I, "but in what way am I affected by it?"

' "It is no fairy tale, dear lady, I assure you. I will not bore you with the details of my researches, but I can promise you that the story of the red powder and its value to medical science is quite true. There was little enough of it when Kelley first discovered it, so there may only have been a few grains remaining when he finally hid it away. The last seven years of my life have been devoted to locating the spot where that vial was buried. Having followed certain hints found in Eckermann's *Alchemy and Britannic History*, I can now say with tolerable confidence that that spot is somewhere on the grounds upon which Field House presently stands. I propose – with your permission, of course – to conduct an archaeological dig on your property. With the assistance of my fellow scholars, I estimate that the endeavour should take no more than a week. To prevent your experiencing any inconvenience during this time, I have arranged for you to spend the week at one of the hotels on Northumberland Avenue in London. I recommend that you dismiss your servants for that same period; I can see no reason for their staying on when the lady of the house is not in residence."

'I had felt it only polite to allow this Mr Valentine to speak his piece but I had begun to weary of his tomfoolery.

' "Mr Valentine," I said, firmly, "thank-you for the time you have taken to call upon me with your interesting request, but I regret to inform you that it holds no attraction for me whatsoever. I wish Field House and its environs to remain undisturbed."

'To my surprise, he did not seem at all disappointed by this setback. "I can see that it would be useless to ask you to reconsider, madam," he said, "but I cannot stress the importance of this matter sufficiently, not only to the public at large, but to yourself in particular."

' "But I am quite well, Mr Valentine," I responded.

' "And I pray that you remain so. Your refusal makes me very sad. Very sad indeed."

'Feeling somewhat unnerved by his remarks, I rang for Peter, who escorted the gentleman off the property. It was as I heard the door close behind him that I was struck by a sudden realization – he had not been striding to the window and back out of some sort of nervous agitation, as I had thought. *Rather, he had been watching for a confederate waiting outside the house.*'

'You say someone? Might it not have been some*thing*?' Holmes queried.

'No, Mr Holmes, for I was just in time to see the two of them together by the beech tree.'

Holmes rose and strode to the window. I followed, not wishing to appear disinterested and hoping to observe something of significance. But, save from confirming that Mrs Cartner could indeed have watched two men in conversation under the large beech tree just outside the gate, I could see nothing.

'Unfortunately, the other man remained in the shade and I could see little of him, save that he was about a head shorter than Mr Valentine, who was not himself a tall man. His hair was black, I believe, but I could not swear to it. They spoke for about two minutes, my visitor frequently gesticulating and glancing at the front of the house. Stood at the window as I was, I do not know how he could have failed to see me.'

'A singular occurrence, to be sure,' Holmes observed, returning to his chair. I waited a moment longer, on the off chance that a clue might suddenly appear to me, but disappointed, I resumed my seat also.

'You do not strike me, Mrs Cartner, as the sort of person who would allow themselves to be frightened by such an incident,' said Holmes. 'What has happened since then?'

'Your confidence in my nerve is gratifying, Mr Holmes, but I must confess that for some reason I had the idea of contacting you immediately after my meeting with Mr Valentine. However, it seemed such a trivial matter that I immediately put the idea out of my head. The next afternoon, I was visiting a sick neighbour, when the fellow called again. He came to the kitchen door claiming to be a representative of a London auctioneer's. From the description given by the maid it could only have been Basil Valentine. He claimed that he had been summoned to value several items of property. Obviously, the rogues had discovered the details of my situation, not it that would have been difficult for them to do so. The girl had no instructions from me in this regard and thought it peculiar that anyone calling upon the lady of the house should knock at the servant's entrance. Growing impatient with her uncertainty, Mr Valentine then produced a pound note from his pocket.

' "Look here, my girl," he said, "this money is yours if you will allow me half an hour without interruption inside the house. When I leave, you may have the same amount again."

'Frightened, the maid called for Peter the footman, at which point Valentine fled, scrambling over the hedge and disappearing. He has not called again, but I have been aware of figures prowling about the outskirts of my property at various times of the day. In one instance, I was alarmed by a sudden crash and discovered that the stone sundial in the garden had been tipped over, presumably by accident. I was more or less certain at that moment that I would engage you on this matter, but Peter's experience two nights ago decided me on this course of action. Perhaps you would care to hear it from his own lips.'

Before she had a chance to ring for the intimidating servant, the girl entered the sitting room with our tea. I felt a twinge of unease at the remembrance of my earlier *faux pas*. Mrs Cartner asked the maid to summon Peter, and less than a minute after her departure the fellow was standing over us, appearing no less fearsome than he had upon our arrival. I wondered whether, with his military baring, he had seen service at some point. However, following Holmes' somewhat shoddy treatment of my deductive capabilities that morning, I decided against asking his opinion.

'With the events of the last few days,' Peter began, 'I have been reluctant to leave the mistress alone at home.'

'However, I insisted,' Mrs Cartner interrupted. 'Peter has been on the alert for intruders for some days now, and I was quite adamant that he take a well-deserved respite. It was not an easy matter to persuade him, however, and he eventually agreed on the condition that he not be away from the house for more than an hour. Please continue, Peter.'

'I spent that hour in the local hostelry, *The Dutch Masters*. I was sitting alone when that blighter slid into the chair next to me. I should have had him by his collar and marched him to the police station that very moment, but the scoundrel had the gift of the patter alright and he started up before I even realised he was there.'

' "You would probably like to see me up to my neck in the river," he says, "and I can't say that I blame you. This whole business has been shockingly badly managed, and I promise you that that was not my idea. I don't take pleasure in distressing – uh, pardon me, ma'am – childless widows. That is why I am putting a stop to it here and now, and to do that I need your help, sir."

' "If that's the case," I asks, "then why the devil – pardon me, ma'am – do you need my help and why the- what makes you suppose that I would be willing to help you?"

' "I don't see that your employer need be troubled at all, Mr- Tierney, is it? All I ask of you is that tomorrow you deliver a note into her hands that will draw her away from Field House for a short time. Then you and the rest of the staff may enjoy a pleasant lunchtime in this establishment, and when you return to your duties, everything will be as it was before, so far as you can tell. Mrs Cartner will never see or hear from me again. How do you like the sound of that, eh?"

'Well, I've met plenty of fancy talkers in my time and I never trusted a one of them. I made a grab for the rascal's coat, but he was just a little too fast for me, and he was out of his chair and through the door of the pub before I'd even got up. Ten years ago, or even five, I'd have caught up with him, right enough.'

'Peter did not wish to upset me with an account of the incident,' Mrs Cartner added, 'but I swear that I can always tell when something is troubling him and I soon got the whole story out of him. He has a charming lack of affectation in that regard. Thank-you, Peter, that will be all for now. After he told me the tale, I finally put pen to paper, as I had meant to do for some time. Forgive me, Dr Watson, if my insistence that you accompany Mr Holmes caused you any inconvenience-'

I shook my head vigorously.

'-But by this stage I was so excessively nervous that I imagined these people, whoever they are, might be capable of intercepting my letters. If a risk existed that they could do so and send impersonators in your stead, I thought that if I were adamant that you both come they would be less likely to find suitable doubles at short notice. Hence my relief upon seeing, doctor, that you are just as you are depicted in the *Strand* Magazine, moustache and all.'

For perhaps the first time in the long period of our acquaintance, Holmes appeared ill at ease. 'A small confession then, ma'am. Although Dr Watson did indeed pose for those drawings, I expressed an unwillingness to participate, and I understand that the artist used his brother, Sidney Paget-'

'Walter,' I corrected.

'-Walter, thank-you, Watson – as a replacement. I am told that we are not dissimilar in appearance. But to return to the matter of your peculiar persecution, you say that you have often been aware of these intruders during the day, Mrs Cartner. Has there ever been any sign of them at night?'

'Why, no.'

Holmes eyes glistened and I recognised the look of satisfaction he wore when he was on the right scent. 'Then if I have your permission, and if Dr Watson has finished his tea, we will examine the grounds. Please make a start without me, Watson, I wish to have a brief word with Peter.'

3. I THEORIZE

I was alone in the garden for several minutes. The day remained fair and the heat of the late afternoon sun tingled on my neck most pleasurably. It would have been quite easy to forget for a moment that I was patrolling the grounds of a house under siege. The charming and personable Mrs Francis Cartner was relying on us, and I did not intend to see her disappointed. With this intention in mind, I got down on all fours and began examining the grass minutely.

'Watson, your ungainly pose will almost certainly have obliterated any traces upon that spot.' I looked up to see Holmes, his stick in one hand, his other outstretched. 'Let me help you up. I wished to discuss a few matters with Peter and he is presently dispatching telegrams on my behalf. We must hold off any invasion together until he returns. His employer was quite effusive in her apologies regarding the quality of her stationary. If you are quite satisfied that there is nothing to be learned here, shall we continue?'

As we made our way around the grounds, I was occasionally aware of our client watching us from the house.

'You have an admirer, I think, Watson. A very attractive woman, is she not?'

'Is she?' I said, languidly. 'I did not observe.'

'Oh, come, Watson! Your indifference surprises me. After all, I am indebted to you for the fact that I now acknowledge a pretty face when I see one.'

'I am very pleased to hear you say so, Holmes.'

'Yes, I freely admit that it was foolish of me not to allow for the importance of physical attractiveness as a factor in the commission of a crime. I have been involved in several investigations over the years where a problem may hinge on an individual's weakness for a beautiful woman. You will recall, Watson, the adventure of the Unpowdered Nose.'

'Should I ever decide to write it up, I'm sure I shall pick a better title than that,' I responded, testily.

My aggravation was not due solely to Holmes' manner but also to his apparent disinterest in the problem at hand. On more than one instance I had seen him lie flat upon his face, searching for evidence, but now – despite the trust placed in us both by an anxious and gracious lady – he did little more than poke at the untended grass with his stick.

'I count at least three persons so far,' he said, at last, 'none of them the manservant Peter, whose left foot is at least a size larger than his right. Does it strike you as peculiar, Watson, that a man should manage to knock over a heavy stone sundial in broad daylight?'

'Perhaps he thought he had been observed and simply panicked,' I suggested.

'Watson, your dogged refusal to eliminate even the impossible is a continual source of astonishment to me.'

This last jibe was, I felt, quite the wrong side of too much and I took my companion to task. 'Holmes, all morning you have derided my attempts to put into practice your theories on the science of deduction, theories upon which I might say I have expanded considerably over the passing years.'

Holmes raised a quizzical eyebrow.

'For instance,' I continued, 'I have formed my own opinion regarding our client's unnerving experience and I venture to suggest that my theory fits the facts as we know them.'

Holmes slumped back against the nearest tree. 'Pray enlighten me, doctor.' I was pleased to note that I did not detect even a trace of mockery in his tone.

'It seems to me evident that this story of the red powder buried somewhere in the vicinity is nothing more than a flimsy concoction of Valentine's, intended to mask some sinister purpose.'

'I am certainly in agreement with you on that point, Watson, but there is at least some historical basis for the story of Edward Kelley, although he lived considerably earlier than Valentine claims. Many properties, including the bestowing of the ability to commune with the angels, have been ascribed to the fabled red powder – which he came by in Wales, by the way, not Berkshire. I am unaware of any work by Eckermann suggesting that it might be located in these parts. Indeed, I do not believe Kelley ever visited this area in his life.'

'As I say, merely a ruse in order to gain entry to Field House, a motive made clear by the later unsuccessful attempts. Incidentally, Holmes, I *am* quite aware that Edward Kelley was a real person, in fact I am certain that our adversary's scant research into the subject suggested his own *alias* to him - Basilius Valentinus was a sixteenth century Benedictine who published a treatise on alchemy. No doubt that is why you thought his name familiar. You need not appear so astonished, Holmes, you are not the only person with access to the reading rooms of the British Museum, you know.'

In truth, although I had been quite offhand about the matter, I was extremely satisfied at the effect my words had upon Holmes, who – after a moment or two of uncertainty – emitted a sharp bark of a laugh.

'You do well to chide me, Watson! Our client's agreeable nature seems to have had a remarkable effect on your cognitive abilities – I would go so far as to say that you positively scintillate this morning. Very well then, what do you suppose was the reason for our Mr Valentine's error regarding the time in which Kelley lived?'

'Oh, that! Simply a mistake on the blackguard's part, I imagine. I ascribe no importance to it whatsoever.'

Holmes smiled a tight-lipped smile. 'I see. Please continue, Watson. What do you suggest is the sinister purpose for which Valentine and his associates wish access to Mrs Cartner's home?'

'Evidently, there is something hidden in that house which is of great value to them and which Mrs Cartner does not realise she even possesses.'

'And what might that item be, pray?'

'Ah, there I am at a loss, I am afraid. I am loathe to theorize without data, you see-'

'Watson, does it occur to you that we are witnessing a curious parallelism of events? A visitor presents an improbable scenario, when rejected he resorts to menacing promises of disastrous consequences...'

I frowned as Holmes described the sequence of events. Put that way, they did seem curiously familiar.

'The missing papers of ex-President Murillo!' I gasped.

Holmes merely nodded. 'But how is it that a matter on which you are consulted mere weeks ago should play a part in our present investigation? Surely that is more than coincidence!'

'I admit that there are some features of this case that are not yet clear to me, but I hope to have them clarified by tomorrow. In the meantime, Watson, you are doing so well that I think it would be nothing short of criminal to rob you of the credit for discovering the missing memoirs and

I therefore put you in charge of the investigation from this point on and place myself entirely at your disposal. Your instructions will be followed to the letter. Now, where do you propose we begin our search?'

4. AN INFLUENTIAL VISITOR

I first learned of the Murillo matter some two weeks earlier, when I was still in residence at my Kensington practice. Although I had long since abandoned the habit of sleeping late, as I had done so often when still a bachelor and in most respects carefree, one Saturday morning in May I somehow failed to rise at my usual hour. Donning an unnecessarily thick dressing-gown for the time of year, I wandered the house, eventually entering my study where I discovered Sherlock Holmes seated at my writing desk, skimming through a draft copy of my account of the involvement of Professor Moriarty in the outrages known to the public as the Jack the Ripper crimes. Although the full facts of the matter may never be known, some readers – Inspector Tobias Gregson among them – will be aware that it was on a balcony high above the streets of London that Holmes was able to remove a plague-spot from the Whitechapel area.

'You will never be allowed to publish this, you know,' said Holmes, holding one of the pages aloft while still poring over another. 'Too many reputations, including that of an innocent woman, would be damaged.'

I stepped over to the desk, removed the paper from my visitor's hand and replaced it in its proper order in the pile on the desk. 'I had already reached that conclusion,' I replied, 'after receiving a strongly-worded letter from the brother of Professor Moriarty.'

'Which one?'

'James.'

'Ah. Forgive the hour, Watson, but I was re-acquainting

myself with the mud stains of the Kensington area and decided to pop by. I told your maid not to wake you on my account.'

In the weeks following his dramatic return, Holmes had made a habit of appearing unannounced at my door. It was often so in the past, of course, although I can recall only one occasion – during his investigation of the supposed murder of Colonel Barclay in '88 – when he stayed under my roof overnight. But now, for some unaccountable reason, his visits filled me with dread. I dared not say anything of the sort to Holmes, of course, and if he had deduced it from my unconscious actions he did not say so. I could only hope that my unease would abate once I found myself back at Baker Street.

'And how goes the sale of your practice?' Holmes asked at last.

I lowered myself into the chair usually reserved for patients and noticed for the first time how uncomfortable it was. 'Surprisingly well, in fact,' I replied, 'Dr Verner has expressed no opposition to the sum I have requested, although I confess it seems to me far too high.'

'Then you should raise it. I am certain the doctor's capital is as good as his name.'

I considered Holmes' curious recommendation as the maid entered, bearing a tray of coffee things. I hastily rearranged my dressing gown as she placed the tray on the desk beside Holmes.

'Why, thank-you, Megan,' said Holmes, charmingly. Although I never knew him to have close relationships with females, he appeared to exude a certain allure when he chose. 'And perhaps a cup for the doctor?'

The maid curtsied and left the room, not to be seen again for the remainder of the morning.

'It's a strange thing,' I remarked as Holmes poured his cup of coffee and I pondered the furnishings, 'but my practice has been all that I have existed for during these past few years, but in a matter of weeks I shall be abandoning it utterly.'

'I am very glad of it,' Holmes said, after taking a tentative sip. 'I did not rise from the dead, so to speak, in order to resume a solitary existence.'

I did not pursue the point, but Holmes' remark addressed a problem that had been troubling me of late; why, having returned to London to orchestrate the capture of Colonel Sebastian Moran, had he elected to remain? More than once had he told me that he considered that his career would be over following the arrest and execution of Professor Moriarty. But the so-called Napoleon of Crime had been dead these three years, and yet here was Sherlock Holmes, back in his Baker Street lodgings of old and on the brink of resuming his career as a consulting detective. Looking back, I imagine that I shied away from the subject out of a fear that he might simply vanish again, leaving my life in even greater chaos. Instead, I asked whether he had yet accepted any cases.

'I regret to say that the level of public interest has been somewhat disappointing. The natural cynicism of the Londoner, I suspect, leads him to believe that reports of my return to life have been greatly exaggerated. However, I have hopes, my boy. Why, only yesterday, I turned away a representative of the San Pedro government. You recall San Pedro, I trust?'

'I should say that I do and with good reason. Who could forget the brutal crimes committed by Henderson, alias ex-president Murillo, "The Tiger of San Pedro" at Wisteria Lodge? The country is doing so well without him, I hear, that I am considering making a small investment in its future.'

'You interest me exceedingly, Watson, please tell me more. Oh, before you proceed, I should inform you that the phrase "The Tiger of San Pedro" has fallen out of favour in his home country, where the preferred term is now, I understand, "The Hanging Tyrant". Incidentally, his brutal crimes were actually committed at High Gable, not Wisteria Lodge. And I believe you mean *Wistaria* Lodge, do you not?'

I grimaced, but, deciding against attempting to argue these minor points, I simply continued my explanation, rubbing my forefinger and thumb together thoughtfully as I spoke. 'I have been advised by a chap at my club that there is money to be made from the San Pedro tin mining industry. He assures me that with sufficient backing from the state as well as a few discriminating investors, San Pedro could become the largest manufacturer of tin in the western world.'

'Excellent, Watson. I'll make you my handy guide to the stock market should the need arise. But will the profits from your sale of the practice not be sufficient for your simple wants?'

'One must have money in order to make money, Holmes,' I informed him, perhaps a little more brusquely than was necessary. 'The first rule of commerce.'

'I consider myself instructed. But Mr Santini – that was my visitor's name – called upon me regarding a matter of greater moment than the tin mining business.'

'And yet you say you sent him away?'

'I distrusted him from the start. This is excellent coffee, by the way, old fellow.' He drained his cup and replaced it on the saucer.

'I am delighted to hear it. Was it some deduction you made based on his appearance that caused you to distrust him?'

'That was just the point, Watson. For the very first time in my career, I have met a man about whom I could reach no conclusions whatsoever. His clothes were neat enough and expensive enough, but there were no identifying features about them, no traces of the wearer's individuality. This Santini was a study in practised anonymity. There is no doubt, however, that he is exactly what he says he is, an agent of the San Pedro government, but I regret to say that I was able to ascertain this fact only by communicating with my brother Mycroft at his Whitehall office. I certainly hope that my talent for observation and inference has not deserted me during my travels; the day may yet come when I am forced to go through a client's pockets in order to form any conclusions about him.'

'Never, Holmes,' I reassured him.

'You are kind to say so, Watson. For much of the interview, Santini alternated between an ingratiating cherubic grin and an aspect of funereal seriousness that I must admit I found almost comical. It was with the former expression that he sang my praises.

' "Mr Holmes," he began, "may I say what a sincere pleasure it is to shake hands with the man who defied the Hanging Tyrant himself, Don Juan Murillo."

' "My part in the affair was a very small one, Mr Santini, and I cannot say that I was at all satisfied with the outcome," I replied.

' "But all has worked out for the best. Indeed, I am proud to say that I was one of the crowd who cheered so enthusiastically that glorious day when the brown and yellow flag of the old San Pedro was taken down from the palace roof and replaced with the green and white flag of the new, democratic San Pedro. An inspiring day, Mr Holmes. Like so many, I believed that following Murillo's death - no doubt the result of a falling-out with his confederates - my homeland would be forever free of his tyranny."

' "But something has happened to change all that," I suggested.

' "I have received certain disquieting information from San Pedro that could put at risk all that we struggled so hard and for so long to achieve." As he spoke, Watson, the benevolence all but disappeared from Santini's face, and he adopted an air of excessive solemnity in his attempt to convey to me the seriousness of the situation. "It seems that, during his time in your country, the Hanging Tyrant dictated his memoirs to his secretary Lopez, the man you knew as Lucas."

' "I knew him not at all, Mr Santini. I am sorry to say that both Lopez and his master escaped not only my clutches, but also those of the very capable Inspector Baynes." Holmes broke off from his reminiscence and turned to face me. 'By the way, Watson, do you know anything of Murillo's death?'

I felt somewhat ashamed at this unexpected question, like a disobedient schoolboy, for in all the uproar following Holmes' return to London, I had completely forgotten to tell him what I had learned of the outcome of our adventure. I began to feel even more physical discomfort than before as I explained: 'Inspector Baynes wrote to me about it,' I replied. 'It happened in Madrid, about six months after you... about six months after. Murillo and Lopez were both discovered stabbed in their rooms at the Hotel Escurial. Definitely *not* the result of a falling out, Baynes says. Knowing your high regard for the fellow's gifts, I feel certain that you would have agreed with his conclusions.'

Holmes mulled over this new information for a short while before reacting. 'A most unsatisfactory ending for your readers, Watson.'

'I may make a few changes if I ever decide to write it up.' He gave me his most disapproving gaze, which he usually reserved for discussions concerning my literary ventures. 'You said yourself that I would not be able to relate the affair in my usual style.'

'Did I? Hm. I do not recall. How is Baynes, by the way?'

'I regret to say that he has not been as successful in his career as you predicted. He is working in Sheffield at the moment, I believe, but he still has hopes of one day receiving his transfer to Scotland Yard.'

Holmes shook his head, regretfully. 'He will not get it. The Yard is fearful of his imagination and intelligence. It is their way, and I am saddened to learn that it has not altered these last three years. But to return to my story, I pressed Santini for details regarding these memoirs of which he spoke.

' "It is understood that within this valuable document, which has yet to be located, the cursed Murillo has named several members of the current government who are loyal to his cause."

' "And you wish me to trace it for you?" I began to rummage in my dressing gown for my black clay pipe as I spoke, for I was beginning to lose my enthusiasm for this interview. "I have been away from polite society for several years, Mr Santini, but it seems to me that this is hardly a matter of the greatest moment-"

' "*But it is!*" he cried. And I must confess, Watson that so taken aback was I by the unexpected ferocity of his interruption that I dropped the pipe, which then rolled beneath my chair. "The future of San Pedro rests on the recovery of the- of those papers." As suddenly as it had arrived, the storm subsided and he returned to his beatific persona of a few moments earlier. He brushed an imaginary speck of dirt from his trousers and resumed in a calmer tone. "Should any of these men choose to follow his path, San Pedro could once again find herself under the thrall of a second Murillo. As long as they hold positions of power and influence, they are a threat to democracy. They have no place in our government or in our country, to say nothing of this life and the next. I hope I make my position clear, Mr Holmes?"

' "Abundantly, Mr Santini," I replied, hoping that my sense of unease could not be detected in my speech. I decided that it would make a poor impression were I to attempt to retrieve my pipe at that moment. "But surely the… friends of democracy had an agent within the

Murillo household. Could not she tell you where the papers are to be found?"

' "Regrettably, Signora Durando entered the employment of Mr Henderson - as he was then known - after the notes had been dictated. She dared not pursue the matter for her position as governess was a tenuous one at best. It took a great deal of persuasion to induce Miss Stoper to place a governess of limited accomplishments with such an affluent family."

'I did not say so at that moment, of course, but it occurred to me that the accomplishments of the woman we knew as Miss Burnett were truly remarkable in areas other than the purely educational. Not only did she operate as a spy in an enemy's territory, she also planned and played a part in two assassination attempts, the latter successful. I think that, knowing what we do now, we may place the responsibility for the deaths of Murillo and Lopez squarely at her door.'

'I even think that she would even feel gratified were she to hear you say so,' I suggested.

'Phaedrus puts it best, I think - *Saepe intereunt aliis meditantes necem.*'

'I believe the Chinese have a similar saying about digging two graves,' I offered, not wishing to be left behind.

Holmes chuckled. 'I see we still have much to teach one another, Watson. That is very good. Well, Santini went on to clarify the situation for me.

' "I have been assured by the associates of Miss Burnett," he said, "that these treasured papers were not stored at High Gable or anywhere in the vicinity. They have been quite thorough on this point. However, there is a limit to how far they can operate effectively in a country not their own, and, despite their zeal, they lack the skill of the seasoned investigator. All that is required of you, Mr Holmes, is to trace Murillo's movements in England in the period before he was identified under his alias of

Henderson, and then to clarify where the manuscript is hidden. You will then advise me of the fact, and I shall make appropriate arrangements for its recovery. I would also appreciate a detailed accounting of your expenses."
' "You go too fast, sir," I interjected, raising my hand in a placating gesture. "This is a matter in which – to employ the term favoured by an associate – the old hound is the best. I am hardly the most suitable agent to act on your behalf in this business. There are few of the opportunities for logical deduction that I require in order to hold my attention."
'Santini appeared more aghast than infuriated by my refusal. "But, Mr Holmes. I assumed that as a friend of democracy-"
' "As a friend of democracy, sir, I advise you to seek assistance elsewhere. Here in London we have lots of Government detectives and lots of private ones. I even understand that I am no longer the only unofficial consulting detective. Indeed, you might do a good deal worse than to employ a young man named Frederick Darnay, who has studied my methods quite closely. I am certain that he would be better suited to the task. Who knows, he might even provide you with a detailed accounting of his expenses. Now, if you will excuse me, before your arrival I was in the process of organising my files, which, I am sorry to say, have got quite out of order in my absence. Good-day to you, sir."
'I am uncertain whether or not I am acting rashly, Watson, but we must all make sacrifices for our art, and that is mine.'
'And it sounded so promising!' I groaned.
'Bah! The mere show of detective work. Where are the features of uniqueness upon which I pride myself?'
'But have you not said yourself that some of your most interesting cases have arisen from the observation of trifles?'

My irrational annoyance at Holmes' cavalier attitude must have been evident either in my manner, for his reply was in the calm and measured tone one might employ with a fractious child. 'I am not retained by the San Pedro secret police to supply their deficiencies, Watson. For all its implications of international intrigue, this is so transparent an affair even a Scotland Yard official could clear it up. I would be happy to pour you the remainder of the coffee, Watson, but I am afraid that it has gone cold in the pot. There is only one small mystery provided by the encounter, and that is why Mr Santini should presume to lie to me.'

'To lie?'

'I found his story of the Hanging Tyrant's memoirs improbable on two counts. I may be out of touch with modern political practice, but it seems peculiar to me that the discovery of the existence of a list of potential traitors made in San Pedro should not lead in due course to their exposure.'

I considered the likelihood of this. 'Caesar's assassins perished after Mark Anthony's speech,' I offered.

'A daring metaphor, Watson! But there is another reason for supposing Santini's claim to be a fabrication. When he became agitated at my lack of interest - a response that, I am sorry to say, I appear to provoke in others – I am certain that he came perilously close to disclosing the true nature of his mission. I have a very strong rule about permitting mystery at only one end of my cases; I would not break it for the Prime Minister and I see no reason to break it now.'

I shrugged wearily, and rose to replace the coffee things on the tray in the hope that the maid might discover them and return them to the kitchen. Holmes glanced up at what he must have assumed was a sorrowful mien.

'Do not despair, old fellow,' he said. 'I should be very surprised if we do not hear from our mysterious Mr

Santini again.'

'What makes you say that, Holmes?' I asked.

'The unsettling nature of his departure. After my somewhat brusque refusal of his request, he rose slowly from his chair like an invalid. He trembled, and the action changed from one of premature frailty to barely repressed rage. He retrieved his cane, turned and held it out before him like a weapon, ramrod straight, with the iron ferrule only inches from my nose.

' "You have made a terrible mistake this day, Mr Holmes," he said, his voice quivering with fury. "You have held many lives in your hands and you have abandoned them all."

'I saw no reason to prolong the interview by responding and thereby inflaming his passions further. He left without saying another word, and I retrieved my pipe at my leisure. It seems to me that I have been threatened in those rooms many times over the years, but I promise you Watson that it is only through Santini's obscure words that I have experienced a genuine sense of menace. I cannot believe that too much time will pass before we discover their meaning.'

5. AN UNEXPECTED DEVELOPMENT

In the course of my long and fruitful association with Mr Sherlock Holmes, I have seen rediscovered many valuable items which were believed to be lost forever. I was not, however, under the impression that the search for the missing papers of ex-President Murillo would be a simple one. Although not an enormous dwelling, Field House was certainly a sizeable property containing many rooms. A thorough search of all of them might last well into the next morning. In addition to this, I was all too aware that Holmes had chosen that moment to place his reliance in my abilities. I felt considerable pride at the thought that he believed me capable of uncovering the hiding place of these documents, and I did not wish to disillusion him by failing to locate it.

Our first port of call was the library, where I began to examine with great care the titles on the shelves. After a few minutes of silence, I became aware that Holmes, still standing in the doorway, was growing impatient.

'May I ask the point of this exercise, Watson?'

'We both know, Holmes, that secret passages are the stuff of romantic fiction. However, we have discovered more than one hidden room in our time. I need hardly remind you of the supposed murder of Mr John Douglas, I suppose? Or of the terrifying experience of Miss Grace Farrington? Or even of the horrifying incident at Arnsworth-'

'The point is well made, Watson,' Holmes snapped. 'But what has this to do with our client's choice of reading matter?'

'Well, I hoped that I might find a history of Field House here, describing the inclusion of some concealed chamber during construction.'

'And have you?'

'No.'

'Of course, in certain examples of romantic fiction, a particular book on a shelf is often merely a lever that opens a door hidden behind the bookcase.'

I reflect on this for a moment. It was certainly improbable, but by no means impossible. Of course, the way to find the correct book would surely be to identify an appropriate title. Not *The Future of the Argentine*, surely, nor *Mirror of Society*. My eyes ran across volumes including *The Clue of Crimson* and *Sport in the Rockies*, no doubt purchased by the late Mr Cartner.

'It is worth adding in this particular instance,' Holmes observed, 'that if this bookcase *were* a hidden door, it would lead only into the sitting room, which is directly behind that wall.'

I sighed, before setting my shoulders straight and adopting a determined air. 'Then I suggest we begin a room-by-room search of the premises. We will start upstairs and work our way down.'

As I had feared, the task went on for many hours, with Holmes unwilling to offer any suggestions of his own or to search without instruction. A grateful Mrs Cartner kept us provided with refreshments, but I was becoming more and more dispirited and concerned that our client's faith in us would begin to wane.

It was growing dim, and I was slumped against a wall with fatigue and frustration, when a thought suddenly struck me.

'Holmes,' I said. 'We have been fools.'

'Have we? Do go on, Watson.'

'Why have Valentine and his allies waited until this moment to approach Mrs Cartner?'

'An excellent question, Watson. One that no doubt strikes at the very heart of the matter.'

'I suggest that whatever these persons desire, the lady unknowingly brought here with her. It was not in the house prior to her arrival, rather it is secreted somewhere about the expensive furniture in the sitting room. No doubt that is why Valentine posed as an auctioneer upon his second visit, so that he might study these items.'

Holmes made no reply, from which I gathered that he was quietly impressed with my display of logic.

'There's not a moment to lose, Holmes!' I cried, feeling a sudden resurgence of my original enthusiasm. 'The game's afoot!'

The thrill of the hunt had quite revived me, and I now understood what it meant to Holmes to be hot on the scent. But, alas, it proved not to be so. Despite a quite thorough examination of all the items in the sitting room – performed under the watchful eye of Peter, who was determined to see that none of his mistress' property was in any way marked or damaged – the papers were not unearthed. I was quite disconsolate, unable to see where my deductions had been at fault. To make matters worse, Mrs Cartner – who by this stage insisted that I refer to her as Violet – had been present at what I hoped would be my triumphant moment. She hid her disappointment skilfully, which only made my shame greater. Holmes was of little help, suggesting only that he and I should retreat to a nearby inn for the night and approach the problem fresh in the morning.

'Contrary to Dr Watson's exercises in romantic fiction, matters are not always quite so easily worked out,' he advised our client. Violet Cartner nodded in reply and wished us both a restful night.

I was extremely glad that Holmes could not be persuaded to remain in Field House for I do not think I could have continued to look into the lady's eyes, imagining that I could see in them intense disillusionment.

As we sat over a meal at *The Dutch Masters*, Holmes seemed suddenly to become aware of my gloomy disposition.

'Do not be so downhearted, old friend. I am certain that events will reach a satisfactory conclusion in time for me to make my appointment in Bedfordshire tomorrow. Now that we are on the case, Valentine and his compatriots can have no more interest in Field House. We will have ample time to clear this business up.'

The night I spent in my room at the hostelry was, if anything, worse than the last night spent under my own roof in Kensington. Had it really only been a day ago? So much had gone amiss in that time. I had wished to prove to Sherlock Holmes that my contribution to our partnership might be a valuable one, but instead there had been some flaw in my chain of reasoning, and try as I might, I could not identify it. In the early hours, I had quite made up my mind that I would inform Holmes that I would not, after all, be joining him at Baker Street. It was clear to me, at least, that I had nothing of any worth to offer in the business of criminal detection and that it would only be a matter of time before Holmes began to weary of my bungling.

At what point during these cogitations I eventually fell asleep, I am unsure, but it was light when a persistent rapping on the door awaked me.

'Watson, stir yourself! There is a trap waiting to take us to Field House. This is a matter of some urgency!'

'Holmes, is that you?' I was somewhat disoriented, expecting to awake either in my own home or at Baker Street and instead finding myself in an entirely unfamiliar room. 'What is wrong?'

'I have made a critical miscalculation, Watson. A murder has been committed in the night.'

6. A SINGULAR REUNION

'Fool that I am! I felt certain that there would be no danger, tonight of all nights! What can it mean?'

These words Holmes spoke to himself, appearing to ignore my presence altogether. Thus far on our journey, Holmes had not so much as looked in my direction, preferring instead to stare straight ahead, appearing more than ever like some dark bird of prey, as though contemplating a point just beyond the horizon.

'Holmes, you still have yet to tell me who has been murdered. Is Violet safe?'

'Mrs Cartner is perfectly well, although somewhat distressed, I imagine. It was from the lady that our message originated. Why did they enter Field House at all? What was the need?'

'Then it is Peter, the footman. He disturbed an intruder and paid for it with his life.' Even as I spoke these words, I found them hard to believe; surely few opponents could have bested Peter in a struggle.

'Nor is it Peter.'

With a stab of guilt, I realized that I had never learned the name of Mrs Cartner's maid, for surely it must be she who lay dead. Poor child, how old could she be?

'Nineteen, I should estimate,' said Holmes, breaking in upon my thoughts. 'No, it is not the maid. The body we are to inspect upon our arrival is that of Mr Basil Valentine.'

As we alighted from the trap a representative of the local police met us. Sergeant Patchett wore a Chinese Gordon moustache that succeeded only in exaggerating his inflated features. Upon seeing us, his cheeks turned pink and he chuckled, as though amused by some private joke.

'Well, by Jove!' he cried, with a cheerfulness inappropriate to the situation, I thought. 'When Mrs *Carter* said it was you, I swore it couldn't be true, but it's you, right enough. Who'd have thought – Sherlock Holmes! And I thought you were just a character in a book, and a dead character at that! I expect to dine out on this for many years to come. And you must be Dr Watson, a pleasure, sir. To think, you're neither of you figments of some feller's imagination – what a laugh!'

We exchanged uncomfortable formalities as briefly as possible, for I was anxious to examine the body and to lend support to Mrs Cartner, for whom the whole affair must have been a terrible shock.

'The lady has been telling me something of the business, Mr Holmes,' said the sergeant, reining his jollity in at last, it appeared. 'It all seems very queer to me, I must say, although I'm sure you solved it in an instant, just by lookin' at the butler's bootlaces! Haw haw!'

'Well, I could not foresee this development, sergeant. I suppose we will never know for certain whether the regret

Valentine expressed to Peter over the matter was genuine or not. Rascal though he undoubtedly was, he surely did not deserve this fate, for I do not believe he ever intended harm to the occupants of Field House. Shall we enter?' As we passed the sitting room I observed our client being comforted by an elderly lady whom I did not recognise, but assumed to be a neighbour. For a moment, I thought of joining them. After all, we were here at the lady's request and it would not only be courteous, but compassionate also. Mary, surely, would have expected nothing less from me. I came to my senses, however, upon recollecting that our previous attempt to assist Mrs Cartner had gone very badly awry, and my incorrect assumptions coupled with Holmes' misplaced certainty that she had seen the last of Basil Valentine had led in some way to these tragic circumstances. Surely I could accomplish more at the scene of the crime. Holmes' masterful cry of 'Watson!' decided me in the matter. The sergeant led us upstairs, bestowing upon us as he did his opinions of Holmes' former cases as though they were nothing more than works of fiction.

'I'm bursting to know how you got out of that dreadful chasm,' he said, 'but whatever you do, don't tell me. I shall enjoy the surprise when I read about it. Body's just along here, gentlemen.'

The weak ray of sunlight emanating from the window at the end of the passage stopped just short of the dark figure sprawled before of us. An hour or so earlier, and he might have been discovered only if one happened to trip over his inert form. Although lay on his chest, Valentine's head was twisted to one side; clearly, Peter had not needed to move the body in order to recognise him from their encounter days before in the bar room of *The Dutch Masters*. He had been a young man, by my estimation not quite thirty. In profile, I recognised the expression I have seen all too often when examining those to whom death has come suddenly: utter disbelief that life had chosen that particular moment in which to cease.

'I'm sure you won't consider it a slight, Mr Holmes,' said the voluble policeman, 'but as soon as I heard this strange story from Mrs *Carter's* lips, I instructed the constable to send a wire to Scotland Yard. Perhaps we'll have Inspector *Lestrayde* on the case with us as well.'

'Inspector *Lestrarde* has duties elsewhere at the moment,' Holmes responded, flatly.

'I am certain, however, that the three of us will be able to arrange matters to Mrs *Cartner's* satisfaction.' I added, feeling an unnecessary resentment toward the officer.

'I'm sure we will, doctor,' Patchett replied, with some hesitation. 'First person to find the dead man was the footman, feller by the name of Peter Tierney. 'Least, I think that's what his name is, I could be wrong.'

The dark clothing worn by Valentine I recognised as the sort favoured by the many burglars and cracksmen I had encountered over the many years of my Baker Street residence. Not black, which Holmes informs is easily detectable even in darkness, but a deep shade of blue. I could tell immediately from the position of the limbs that the man had suffered convulsions in his final moments. As I crouched to get a closer look at the body, the reason became plain.

'A knife has been inserted in the back of the neck, just below the skull. The blade probably pierced the brain. In fact…' I reached into my pocket for a pen and used it to probe the wound.

'Careful, doctor,' said the sergeant, warily.

'It's quite alright,' I assured him. 'Yes, a small piece of the blade broke off upon extraction – no doubt chipped against the skull. Here you are, sergeant. Find a knife with a missing tip to match this fragment and you have your murderer.'

'Excellent, Watson,' said Holmes, without emotion. 'But

this fellow still has one more secret to give up. Do we have your permission to turn the body over, sergeant?' Sergeant Patchett, who appeared to be perspiring freely, nodded slowly. With Holmes' assistance, I rolled the corpse onto its back.

'Good Lord!' I exclaimed, the moment his full face became visible.

'You recognise him also, Watson?'

'I understood from the butler that this chap's name is Basil Valentine,' the sergeant offered.

'He is familiar both to Watson and to myself as Oswald Crawshay, a most adept criminal from a family of blackguards. We encountered him in '87, when he was performing as neat a piece of larceny as I have ever seen under the *alias* Hugo Fitch. His uncle – at whose knee he no doubt learned his formidable housebreaking skills – was suspected of the theft of the Melrose necklace, a problem I was never able to resolve to my complete satisfaction. Crawshay has been used and discarded by the men behind this scheme in the cruellest manner imaginable. His murder is a final, desperate gambit and the cards are in their favour. Sergeant, I leave you in charge of the body. Watson, there is nothing more to be learned here and we have an appointment to keep elsewhere.'

He leapt to his feet and took the stairs at such a pace that he was already out of sight as I rose to follow. Standing at the head of the stairs and looking down into the damp-infested hallway, I could see him no longer, but I fancied that I heard his voice emanating from the sitting room. No doubt he was apprising the unfortunate lady of how matters stood at present. Leaving the local officer appearing somewhat ill at ease, I descended and rejoined my colleague.

'Mrs Cartner,' Holmes was saying as I entered, 'I feel confident in saying that this entire ghastly experience will shortly be over for you. I can assure you that you are in no danger and I expect to be able to provide you with a full explanation of events by this evening. For the moment, however, Dr Watson and I have urgent business in Bedfordshire.'

She appeared somewhat startled at this announcement. 'Bedfordshire? But that is where-'

'I know full well what is to be found in Bedfordshire, I assure you, madam. I will contact you again in due course.'

Mrs Cartner cast aside the consoling hand of her neighbour and rose from her chair. I imagined that she doubtless wore the same seriousness of expression when ejecting the late Crawshay from her premises. 'Mr Holmes, a man lies dead in my home, the victim of an act of violence. After all that has gone on here in the past week, I assure you that I have no intention of remaining here simply to await enlightenment by post.' The elderly lady opened her mouth to speak but managed only to draw breath before our client resumed. 'Mrs Lomar has been very kind in calling upon me so soon after rising from her sick bed, but you have my word, gentlemen, that I will not be satisfied until I witness the arrest of the person responsible for this horrible crime.'

Once again, the depth of this young lady's character and integrity astonished me. I am not entirely certain, but I might even have murmured 'Hear, hear' under my breath. Then, remembering my manners, I gave a nod of acknowledgement to Mrs Lomar, who to my knowledge remained entirely silent during the entire discussion. Holmes bowed his head. 'Very well, Mrs Cartner. You are in the right and I in the wrong. I agree that you have a significant stake in the outcome of this affair, and I will see that you have justice. I regret to say that you must abandon the social niceties and take your leave of Mrs Lomar this instant if we are to make the next train to

Bedfordshire.'

An observer unacquainted with the details of our situation
might – had he looked in upon we three in that railway
carriage - have been mistaken in believing that we had not
been introduced to one another previously and so now
feared to strike up conversation. In truth, each of us had
our own reasons for remaining silent.
Holmes insisted upon humming an unfamiliar tune, the
work of a foreign composer named LaFosse, as he later
informed me. Clearly he did not wish to speak of what
might await us at our destination and I knew him well
enough to realise that it would be pointless to attempt to
draw him out upon the subject.
Mrs Cartner had become troubled at Holmes' mention of
Bedfordshire and could not be drawn into conversation
either. Evidently, there existed some personal association
with this area, although I could not imagine what it might
be, and she was clearly attempting determine the
significance of this connection.
For my part, I feared to speak, lest I embarrass myself
further. I had been guilty of misplaced pride in imagining
that I had arrived at the correct solution, but I no longer
had any understanding of recent events, let alone whether
there indeed existed a link between the plottings of the late
Oswald Crawshay and the missing memoirs of the
Hanging Tyrant, Don Juan Murillo of San Pedro. I had
faced similar discomfiture in the past and I was certain
that my relationship with Holmes would survive my
current disgrace – indeed, I had begun to suspect that he
had been aware of the truth from the very beginning and
had wished only to amuse himself by placing the case in
my hands and observing how far I strayed from the truth.
But Violet Cartner had shown faith in me, and I could not
discard the notion that that faith had been destroyed utterly
by my inaction. I felt the urge to speak to her, but I was

unsure what it would be appropriate for me to say under the circumstances.

After an almost unendurable period of silence, I had composed my thoughts sufficiently and summoned up the nerve to speak, but as I turned to address her I saw that, no doubt overcome by the strain of recent events, she had fallen asleep. I saw no need to disturb her, and what little remained of the journey passed in almost total silence, save for Holmes' incessant humming.

We were pulling into the station when Mrs Cartner was jolted awake by my friend leaping to his feet, exclaiming: 'And here he is, waiting for us! Hello again, Mr Santini!'

7. SHERLOCK HOLMES EXPLAINS

'I must confess that I did not expect to hear from you ever again, Mr Holmes.' Santini was exactly as Holmes had described him several weeks earlier, excessively polite, immaculately dressed and apparently benign. Now, sitting opposite me in a cab bound for the nearby village of Marsden Lacey, he wore a guarded expression on his childlike features. Clearly, he had no idea what Holmes had arranged for us. I wondered whether I wore the same expression.

'First of all, may I say, Mr Santini, that I hope I am not encroaching upon the territory of a fellow investigator by contacting you in this manner.'

Santini waggled a gloved hand. 'By no means, Mr Holmes. My countrymen have continued their investigations following our… consultation, but regrettably, we are no closer to recovering the manuscript.'

'Is this the manuscript of which Dr Watson was telling me?' asked Mrs Cartner, the first time she had spoken since our introduction to the apparently genial foreigner. With uncharacteristic rudeness, Holmes ignored the question. 'I must add that I know the true nature of the item – or perhaps I should say *items* – you seek.'

There was no joy in Santini's smile. 'I knew I had picked the right man when I approached you, Mr Holmes. Very well, so you know. And you know also that it changes nothing. In fact, it makes the hunt more important. Do I take it that we expect make the recovery in this town of Marsden Lacey?'

'You may. And may I take it that you observed the precautions I suggested and have not been followed this time?'

Santini nodded. 'I still cannot believe I could ever have been so foolish. I am a slave to my arrogance, and now a man is dead. A foreigner, admittedly, but the responsibility is mine!'

'There is one last matter to be agreed. Whatever fee you were intending to pay me I wish to be given instead to this lady, minus our expenses, which have not been considerable – train fare and accommodation at a peculiarly-named inn, and payments to my colleague, Mr Darnay for his overnight vigil on my behalf. Is that acceptable?'

The gentleman responded that it was. He appeared a little surprised but otherwise satisfied at the limited payment he would have to make.

I, however, was far from satisfied, being more in the dark than ever. Who was this fellow Darnay, what had been the nature of his vigil, and why did his name sound so familiar? 'Holmes,' I said, 'is I too much to ask that you begin to explain yourself? Have you identified the person behind this tangled web of events?'

'I have. In fact, that person is at this moment present in this coach. Please, Mr Santini, Mrs Cartner, do not glower at one another. I do not refer to either one of you but to my good friend Dr Watson. Incidentally, Watson, I apologise for any remarks of an unfavourable nature I might have made in the past concerning your accounts of my doings. If not for them, this fascinating problem might never have been conceived.'

I was, for a moment, dumbstruck. Then, aware that my companions were considering me in a new light, possibly as some sort of master criminal, I spat out: 'But in what way has all this to do with me?'

'If my investigations were not public knowledge thanks to your arrangement with the editors of *The Strand* Magazine, it would have been exceedingly difficult for Crawshay, *alias* Valentine, to persuade Mrs Cartner to employ my services.'

'This is the man you say has been killed, Mr Holmes?' asked Santini.

'Please, Mr Santini, do not interrupt a lady. Mrs Cartner, you were about to speak.'

'I was about to point out, Mr Holmes, that Mr Valentine did *not* persuade me to contact you. He never even mentioned your name.' I recognised the serious demeanour the lady had worn when remonstrating with my friend a few short hours earlier.

'No madam, he did not. But you told us that you had the notion to write to me after his original visit to your home. His deliberately improbable story was, of course, a blind. But his true purpose lay in the deliberate inaccuracies, which included references to "Baker" – my address – and a brother named John who had been wounded in Afghanistan, clearly intended to suggest my friend and colleague Dr John H Watson. He all but told you to seek my guidance, Mr Cartner.'

'Coincidence, surely?' I protested.

'You remember, Watson, my asking whether you considered Valentine's dating error of any significance? How many years ago did he claim Kelley obtained the miraculous red powder?'

I racked my brains. I began to see dimly what he was

hinting at. 'Two hundred and twenty one!' I exclaimed.
'Precisely. Valentine planted a highly ingenious trail,
intended to direct you to my very door, Mrs Cartner. Were
he still alive, I should congratulate him on a commendably
subtle approach, intended to appeal to a part of your mind
you did not even know existed.'
'I believe that I have read something of the sort in a
medical journal: a German doctor writing about something
he calls the *un*conscious.'
Holmes smiled condescendingly. 'There is very little that
gets past Watson,' he advised our fellow passengers.
'But for heaven's sake, Holmes, why should he wish you
to become involved?' I persisted.
'Dear me, things are getting a little confusing, are they
not? Perhaps it would be best if I recounted the events in
their proper order. Some two weeks ago, Mr Santini
requested my assistance in a matter of location and
recovery. Unbeknownst to him, however, his adversaries,
who wished to know how close he was upon their track,
had followed him to my Baker Street rooms. They too,
you see, were in pursuit of the same goal for a quite
different purpose. When it was realised that Santini was –
as far as they were aware – employing the services of a
renowned consulting detective, they decided to take
whatever action they could to delay me for as long as
possible. They were quite far along with their own
enquiries, and had already ascertained that what they were
looking for had been hidden in a property owned by the
late Mr Francis Cartner for letting purposes, and
unoccupied since his death. That property is to be found in
the town of Mardsen Lacey in the county of Bedfordshire.'
'The other house,' Mrs Cartner almost gasped.
'Of course, these persons could not know that I had in fact
refused Mr Santini's case. Believing that I was engaged to
act on his behalf, it seemed to them only a matter of time
before I followed the trail to Bedfordshire. Wishing to

throw me off the scent, the criminals formulated a desperate plan. They obtained the assistance of a gifted criminal practitioner named Oswald Crawshay who - in the guise of Basil Valentine, Professor of Arcane Antiquities - proceeded to relate to Mrs Cartner a tale even more improbable than your own, Mr Santini.'

Santini shifted uneasily in his seat.

'It was immediately obvious to me that the sole purpose of his implausible story was to convince me that these villains expected to find their objective hidden somewhere in Field House, and not in the second property, which I am advised by your valet Peter, is known as Croftlands. The further acts of annoyance you experienced were intended merely to encourage you to bring me into the affair, hence the pantomime with the deliberately overturned sundial, Watson. All these intrusions occurred during the day so that we might be put off our guard at night, when they had already decided Valentine was to be murdered. My one regret in this case is that I did not foresee that element of their plan. You see, once I had arrived on the scene they had no further use for him. They wished only to delay me, to have me waste as much time as possible at Field House, thus providing them with more time to search Croftlands. The killing of Valentine was simply another element, calculated to confound and impede. Please forgive our elaborate charade yesterday, madam, but it seemed most likely that we were being watched – as proved to be the case – so it was necessary that we made a show of it for at least a day. Dr Watson, knowing that my heart was not really in the enterprise, generously offered to direct our elaborate performance.'

I might have congratulated Holmes for as brilliant a display of logical deduction as I had ever seen had I not been infuriated by his casual maltreatment. I felt aggrieved, and was on the brink of saying so.

'Congratulations, doctor,' said Violet, warmly. 'You had

me quite fooled.'

I smiled foolishly, aware that Mrs Cartner was now considering me with something close to admiration.

'And all this time,' said Santini, excitedly, 'Hector Miras and his confederates have been free to locate the-'

'Hector Miras, eh?' Holmes interrupted. 'Former Ambassador for the government of Don Juan Murillo and, my brother advises me, missing since the coup. I had a suspicion he might be behind all this. To allay your fears, Mr Santini, as well as instructing Mrs Cartner's manservant to issue a telegram to Scotland Yard requesting the presence of Inspector Lestrade and several local constables at Croftlands when we arrive, I also contacted one Frederick Darnay, a promising student of my methods. He has been watching Croftlands all this time and would have contacted me the instant anything of note occurred. You would have done well to engage him as I advised you. And now I see that we are close to our destination. Mrs Cartner, I must insist that – halloa, what the blazes is going on?'

Holmes leaned far out of the cab window, and I feared that he would fall beneath its wheels. I could see nothing from the opposite window, and my attempts to adjust my position in the hope of getting a better view were hampered by Santini, pulling on my coat tails in a frantic effort to make me give up my place. I attempted to swat him away with my free hand, and I can only imagine what Mrs Cartner's opinion of this spectacle must have been. There was certainly some commotion up ahead, but the cries of anger I heard made no sense to me whatsoever. Mercifully, the cab halted at that moment, and Holmes wasted no time in jumping out and haring off. I extricated myself from Santini's grasp, advised our fair client to remain where she was for safety's sake, and followed in my friend's wake. As I alighted, I narrowly avoided being run over by a carriage heading in the opposite direction. I flattened myself against our cab, and, as the other vehicle passed, I was aware of its occupants apparently hurling themselves against the windowless walls and cursing in some foreign language. It was not until the carriage had passed that I observed the metal bars on the door and a pair of small hands attempting determinedly to pull them loose.

Turning, I had very little time to take in the details of Croftlands, save to note that in size and shape it might almost have been a mirror image of Field House; the ivy clinging to the front of this building seemed a touch more alive than that attached to its twin, and row of large and ill-kept conifers fronted the gardens. My attention was swiftly focused upon the heated argument taking place in the driveway between Sherlock Holmes and a stout police official I had no difficulty in recognising immediately.

'Inspector Bradstreet!' I cried. 'You are the very last man I expected to see.'

Bradstreet was visibly aggravated by my friend's reaction to the arrest he had clearly just made. 'Dr Watson,' he said, 'I hope that you too are not going to take me to task over my actions today also. In thirty-two years on the Force I have heard such a thing, to allow an act of burglary to go unpunished.'

A young bespectacled man slightly built, and sporting a brown derby approached, his hands outstretched in an apologetic pose. He could be none other than Holmes' protégée, Frederick Darnay, 'I couldn't stop him, Mr Holmes,' he said. 'I told him your instructions, I told them all-'

'A fine business, when some young pup thinks that he can order a Scotland Yard inspector around. In thirty-two years on the force I never heard such a thing, doctor, not in thirty two years.'

'You need not reproach yourself, Darnay, you have done everything that was asked of you,' Holmes responded, ignoring Bradstreet's outburst. 'Now go home and get some rest. I specifically asked for Lestrade's assistance on this case, at least he knows how to take instruction. Where in Heaven's name is he?'

'In Pangbourne,' Bradstreet replied. 'He got word of a murder there early this morning. Asked me to take over here.'

'Confound the man!' Holmes cursed.

It seemed to me preposterous that we should be engaged in a fierce quarrel in such pleasant surroundings, with the warm sun beating down upon us as it had the day before. I shook my head in bewilderment, and realised that Santini and Mrs Cartner, having ignored my instructions, were now stood on either side of me.

'I must say, Mr Holmes, I had no qualms about taking these men into custody the instant I saw what they were up to. They were a vicious lot, and I'm glad we didn't waste a moment. One of them gave Sergeant Crumley a very nasty cut on the arm with this.' From one of the pockets of his frogged jacket, Bradstreet extracted a bloody knife with a broken tip. I snatched it from his grip.

'Thank-you, inspector,' I said. 'One of your colleagues in Pangbourne will be glad to get his hands on this.'

Bradstreet appeared somewhat bewildered by this, and Holmes took the opportunity to set upon him again. 'The plan was not that those devils be allowed to escape, Inspector, but that they should lead us to our objective. Your impatience may have caused us many days of hard work.'

'I don't know anything about any "objective", Mr Holmes. All I know is that some bloodthirsty foreign swine attacked one of my sergeants with a knife, and behind bars is the best place for 'em.'

'We are just wasting more time!' wailed Santini. 'We must begin searching now!'

Bradstreet noticed our companion for the first time. 'Why,

you look like you might be one of them!' he snarled.
'Steady, Inspector,' I advised. 'Mr Santini is a client – of
sorts – and he has a vested interest in uncovering whatever
is hidden in that house. I suggest that from now on we
direct all our attentions to that problem. Does that
arrangement suit you, Holmes? Inspector?'

'I appreciate your agreeing to remain with us, Bradstreet,'
said Holmes, who had regained his composure by this
time. 'It would be best if an official witness were on hand
to prevent any ill-considered actions.' Here he looked
pointedly at Santini, who was preoccupied considering his
surroundings.
The hallway of Croftlands was somewhat larger than that
of Field House, and I assumed that Mrs Cartner had no
hand in its décor, which I considered in hideous taste.
Even from this limited vantage point, it was clear that
Hector Miras and his associates had wreaked havoc
throughout the house; paintings were pulled from the
walls, sliced to bits and their frames smashed, every item
of furniture lay in pieces, even the banister had been
pulled to the ground and apparently cut up with a saw. Mrs
Cartner said nothing. Her mouth remained open, as though
on the point of emitting an expression of horror, but she
seemed unable even to do this. I placed her hand within
mine, but if she even noticed the gesture, she gave no
indication. Clearly, Croftland's most recent occupants had
had a good deal of time in which to conduct their search,
and they had been quite thorough. I wondered whether
Sherlock Holmes might fare any better.
'Well, Mr Holmes,' said Bradstreet, rubbing his large
hands together, 'it seems pretty clear to me that we are
looking for something that has been secreted somewhere
in this house. From the outside, I imagine there must be a
dozen rooms at least.'
'Fifteen, if memory serves, Inspector,' volunteered our

client.

'Where do you suggest we begin?'

Holmes' eyes shone with the amused exultation he reserved for his moments of greatest confidence.

'I believe that we should begin with a question for the owner of Croftlands. Mrs Cartner, this building appears slightly larger than Field House and is – save for the damage done by your knife-wielding tenants - in no better or worse state of repair to my eye. Why then did you favour one house over the other?'

Demurely, the lady replied: 'A woman's whim, Mr Holmes. The truth is, I detested the wallpaper here and I had not the money to redecorate. Normally, I have no objection to the colour yellow, but the addition of brown stripes I find quite-'

'Hideous?' I suggested.

'Just so, Doctor.' Mrs Cartner graced me with an attractive smile and disengaged her hand from my grasp.

'Was the house always decorated so?'

Santini began to protest about the relevance of this line of questioning, but Holmes silenced him with a raised palm.

'I could not say, Mr Holmes. Mr Sawyer always took care of such matters.'

On his haunches, Holmes began to run his fingers over the paper. We three watched in silence for a good minute before the detective spoke.

'Tell me, Mr Santini,' he asked, 'what are the colours of the San Pedro flag?'

'Why, green and white of course, as any schoolboy knows.'

'And before the ousting of President Murillo?'

'As I have told you, Mr Holmes, brown and yellow-'

Santini came to an abrupt halt. As one, we considered the wallpaper as though it had somehow changed before our eyes. Then, the foreign diplomat hurried to Holmes' side, attempting to gain some purchase at the very edge of the decoration.

'Carefully, if you please, sir,' said Holmes, calmly. 'My client's reward is at stake.'

Both men rose, pulling the paper away from the wall slowly. As it fell before me, I observed attached to its reverse side, several dozen pieces of paper. They were slightly smaller than the English equivalent and the print colour was a deep red, but there was no mistaking the fact that these were bank notes of a high denomination.

'The missing San Pedro treasury,' explained Sherlock Holmes. 'Murillo absconded with it, leaving his country virtually bankrupt. Bradstreet, would you be so kind as to assist Mr Santini in the recovery of this treasure trove? Judging by the extensive use of this paper, there would appear to be a good deal of it.'

'Good Lord!' I cried. 'Holmes, when did you deduce that this is what Santini was truly searching for?'

'You will remember, Watson, that I had suspected he was not in earnest when he called wishing to consult me. But I confess, the truth of the matter did not become plain until Mrs Cartner related Valentine's preposterous tale. Where he had purposely laid hints in his speech, calculated to cause Mrs Cartner to involve me in her largely fictional predicament, Santini did so accidentally, sprinkling his address with words related to financial worth – "valuable", "treasured", and so on. Try as he might, he could not discipline himself sufficiently to expunge all thoughts of the stolen treasury from his mind. In fact, he so far forgot himself at one point as to describe the object of his search as "the notes" – bank notes, in fact, which Murillo stole from his country and stored in this house during the brief period in which he rented it from the representative of the late Mr Cartner. I doubt Santini or his countrymen would find anything remotely amusing in the notion that one of the Hanging Tyrant's final acts should be that of *paper* hanging.'

'But could not the new San Pedro government simply print more money?'

'Which would then become next to worthless if Murillo's hoard ever came to light. The Stockholm Banco caused financial disaster for Sweden in the Seventeenth Century by issuing too many notes. The same problem occurred in France less than fifty years later. Why take such a risk when all that is required is to identify the location of Murillo's reserve? It is certainly more ingenious than a buried chest, and I suppose that we should congratulate him for that. The money is needed desperately in San Pedro. I am advised by a financial expert of my acquaintance that if the promising San Pedro tin mining industry is to succeed, it will require the assistance of the government, as well as a few discriminating investors.'

'And one must have money in order to make money,' I reminded him.

'So I am told. There is, of course, one exception: our client. She has no money at present and yet, if the exchange rate with the San Pedro dollar is good, she will doubtless change from a needy widow to one of the richest heiresses in the country.'

I considered this beautiful young woman as she stood silently watching Bradstreet and Santini frantically tearing the paper from the walls and extracting large handfuls of banknotes. If I had spoken to her at that moment, I do not believe that she would have heard me.

'Really, Watson,' snapped Holmes, 'do not tell me that you were considering making a chivalrous gesture?'

'Do not be absurd, Holmes,' I replied, grimly. 'There will never be a second Mrs Watson.'

'I am delighted to hear it. I did not rise from the dead, so to speak, in order to resume a solitary existence. And now, since no one here will notice our departure, we should return to Baker Street at once. I believe you have some unpacking to do, old fellow.'

THE ADVENTURE OF THE EXTRAORDINARY LODGER

'But Mr Holmes, Katie is simply dying to see you!'

'I really hope it will not come to that, Mrs Hudson,' replied Sherlock Holmes.

Thus far in these memoirs, I may have given the impression that at no time in his career did my friend exercise his great gifts on behalf of our long-suffering landlady. In fact, he was involved in several cases at her request: the persecution of her cousin Mathilda, the murder of her niece Mary's fiancé, and the sinister secret concerning her childhood friends, the Smullets. But the most shocking problem of all brought to our attention by that good woman was undoubtedly that of Mr Theodore Hartnell and his extraordinary lodger.

Mrs Hudson had encountered Katie Whitehall when acting as chaperone at a Christmas dance held for local domestics. Katie had proven to be a most personable young woman, and the two had fallen easily into conversation. When Mrs Hudson heard of the astonishing goings-on in the house at Lancaster Gate where Katie was employed as maid, she determined that not a moment should be lost in presenting the problem to her eminent lodger.

Sherlock Holmes, however, was not easily persuaded. He had recently concluded a wearying investigation into the hideous affair of the Cockroach Emporium and was unwilling to accept another case before New Year. Such was the level of depravity we had exposed in our recent enquiry, in which many innocent men and women had suffered painful and lingering deaths, that Holmes was now beginning to doubt the existence of a deity who could permit such cruelty. I did not, therefore, have high hopes for the prospect of a particularly merry Christmas.

So, while the young maid sat expectantly in Mrs Hudson's

parlour, the redoubtable lady attempted to plead with Holmes on her behalf.

'If you desire to see the problem solved, I told her, I strongly recommend you come to my lodger, Mr Sherlock Holmes. She needs your help, sir!'

'And I appreciate your flattering words, Mrs Hudson, but I simply cannot spare the time at present.'

'Mr Holmes, she is terribly worried about Mr Hartnell. And I know exactly how it feels to worry like that about a person.'

Holmes bowed his head low, either in contemplation or disgrace. 'Yes… yes, I am quite sure that you do.' We all three knew to what Mrs Hudson referred: the arson attack on our rooms during the time of her tenant's feud with the notorious Professor Moriarty, and Holmes' disappearance and subsequent return following a period of several years during which she had believed him murdered. It was a debt that had yet to be repaid. 'Very well, show the young lady up, Mrs Hudson.'

Our landlady vanished and returned with her charge at a rate I would hardly have considered her capable of achieving. Katie Whitehall was a pert young woman of perhaps twenty. Her glittering green eyes were strikingly at odds with her rich chestnut hair. As I took her coat and led her to a chair, I saw that she still wore her maid's uniform.

Mrs Hudson cast a benevolent eye over proceedings from the doorway. I was somewhat surprised when, without a word of warning, Holmes shut the door in her face and slumped into his favourite armchair.

'State the nature of your predicament, Miss Whitehall,' he said, 'and kindly be brief.' For all his apparent brusqueness, I noted that in deference to our young visitor, his old and oily black clay pipe remained unlit on the fireplace.

'I understand that it concerns your employer, a Mr

Hartnell?' said I, taking a seat also.

'That's right, doctor,' she replied. 'Mr Theodore Hartnell of Lancaster Gate. He's always been such a good employer. When my old mum got sick last year, he insisted that I be by her side; I've never forgotten that. But now I think that Mr Fenster's driving him mad and I don't know what to do, I swear I don't!'

'Calm yourself, Miss Whitehall,' I said, soothingly. 'Tell us first about Mr Fenster.'

'He arrived at the house one evening, about two months ago. I'm afraid I don't remember the date. He looked like he might be a clergyman, with that white hair and that smile – how I came to hate that smile! – but it was clear as soon as Mr Hartnell clapped eyes on him that he was terrified of the little man.

' "I've come to stay for the holidays, Theo," he said, " or perhaps a while longer. I haven't decided yet, but I'm certain you won't mind giving up your bedroom for the comfort of a guest."

'Where, then, does your employer sleep?' I asked.

'On a cot in his study. He does not know that I overheard their conversation, and says that his doctor has advised him that he has an unusual condition of the spine, which means that he is unable to sleep in a normal bed. The study is the only room in the house no-on is permitted to enter, not even Mr Fenster.'

'Oh?' said Holmes, appearing to take an interest for the first time.

'There is no great mystery in that, Mr Holmes. My employer has interests in several companies, and conducts most of his business from his study. I only go in there to deliver his meals. The day after Fenster's arrival, I heard the two of them arguing about it.

' "If things are to continue as before, I must be allowed some privacy to work!" Mr Hartnell complained.

' "Very well, Theo,' Mr Fenster replied, smugly. "But only

159

because it pleases me to permit it."

' "Curse you, Reuben Fenster! If I were more of a man…"

' "Ah, but you're not, are you? Goodness, this conversation has quite tired me out. I think I shall retire to my room."

'Mr Fenster delights in doing things to annoy my employer. I recall the time he slid down the banister…'

'Do I take it that, despite his white hair, Mr Fenster is an active man?' asked Holmes.

'I suppose so. For the most part, he stays in his room writing letters. There never was such a one for letter writing as he.'

'What letters are these?' I was glad to see that Holmes' interest had been piqued once again.

'I do not know who they are for. He gives them all to the page, Blatcher, for posting. He has that boy quite under his spell; tells him he'll become a rich man if he just follows instructions.' Katie bit her lip and I wondered whether there might not be some affection between the maid and this page. A similar vulgar intrigue concerning our own page had led to the dismissal of the cook, Mrs Turner.

'Mr Holmes, I do not know what is going on in that house, but it is evil, of that much I am sure!' I feared that the young woman might at last lose her composure and begin to sob. 'When I confided in Mrs Hudson, she seemed so sweet, I had no idea that she was the landlady of a famous detective… I have no money to pay you, but I beg you to help me! Mr Hartnell is a good man and does not deserve what is being done to him!'

'You have done wisely in allowing yourself to be guided by the good Mrs Hudson,' said my friend. 'But have you told me all?'

'Yes, all.'

'Miss Whitehall, you have not. You are screening someone.'

'Why, what do you mean by that?'

Holmes rose slowly from his chair and retrieved his pipe. He did not light it, but simply dropped it into the pocket of his dressing gown.

'Mr Fenster has been in residence at Lancaster Gate for two months. Why now, particularly, should your concerns be any greater? Something has happened, and recently, to cause you to break your silence.'

I leaned forward, but stopped short of taking her hand.

'Come, Katie. You would do well to tell Mr Holmes everything.' Holmes resumed his seat, but did not look in our direction, pretending instead to study the furnishings.

Katie's green eyes had become quite watery. She sniffed loudly. 'Very well, sirs,' she said. 'But I have not spoken of it only because I do not know what it means. It's to do with Blatcher, the page. I said that Mr Fenster has him quite mesmerized. Well, a few nights ago, I saw Blatcher deep in conversation with a tall man in the street. I could not make out his features, for he was quite bundled up, but both Mr Hartnell and Mr Fenster were still indoors, so I know it could not have been either of them.

' "Who was that stranger you were talking to in the street, Russell?" I asked him later.

'To my surprise, he reacted in quite a warm manner.

' "You keep your nose out of it, if you know what's good for you!" he snapped. "There's money coming my way, whatever I choose to do. Now leave me alone – I must think!" '

Holmes was silent for a moment, before saying: 'If we were to call upon your employer this evening, would we find him at home?'

A look of pleasant surprise shone on Katie's features.

'Why, yes, I am certain you would; he never goes out in the evenings. But, Mr Holmes, I beg of you, Mr Hartnell must never know of my part in this.'

'I can promise you that he will not know of your visit here,' I assured her. Holmes remained silent, rapt in

161

thought.

'Thank-you both, gentlemen!' she cried, rising. 'I feel as though a weight has already lifted from my shoulders.'

I saw our new client out of the house, assuring her all the while that the situation would shortly be resolved to everyone's satisfaction and that she should trust in Holmes' wisdom at all times.

When I returned to our rooms, I discovered him puffing greedily on a newly-lit pipe. 'I should be grateful for your views on this matter, Watson,' he said, through clenched teeth. 'You must yourself have formed some theory which will explain the facts to which we have listened.'

'In a vague way, yes,' I responded.

'What was your idea then?'

'It seemed to me obvious that this Reuben Fenster is another Charles Augustus Milverton – a ruthless blackmailer who has Theodore Hartnell under his thumb. The letters the page delivers are undoubtedly blackmail notes.'

'A dozen a day – he must have a prodigious clientèle.'

'Can you suggest another explanation?'

'Not at present. The meeting between the boy Blatcher and this mysterious bundled-up man in the street troubles me as it does Katie. It does not fit with any possible explanation of the facts as we know them, and so must give cause for concern. We might learn more from a meeting with Hartnell, but I am still undecided as to whether I should proceed with the matter.'

'But how can you doubt it? That girl has put her trust in you!'

'It will be difficult, if not impossible, to press Hartnell for details if he is in Fenster's power. I cannot advise him if he attempts to deceive us. But, as you say, that girl... Well, my dear Watson, I leave the final decision in your hands. Shall we take the case?'

I smiled, flattered by Holmes' display of trust. I struggled for a moment with what I ought to say but there was really only one fit reply.

'Goodwill to all men, Holmes – the motto of the firm,' I replied.

My friend vibrated with silent laughter. 'Very well, doctor, your hat and boots – there is not a moment to lose!'

The winter winds were so harsh that the two-wheeler in which we travelled threatened constantly to overturn. It was quite black outside, and I was extremely relieved when we were eventually deposited safely outside Theodore Hartnell's sombre, balconied residence at Lancaster Gate.

'He may refuse to admit us,' I pointed out, pulling my overcoat tighter.

'On more than one occasion during my career in detection, I have taken on the role of a Christmas Caroller - the evening may not be a complete loss.'

It appeared at first that Holmes' prediction might come true - the short, thin-faced lad who answered Holmes' knock advised us that Mr Hartnell was not receiving visitors, nor would he at any time in the future. I wondered whether these instructions were given to him by his employer or by the mysterious Reuben Fenster. With the use of a few coins, however, Holmes was able to persuade the page to take his business card, on the back of which he had scribbled the word "Blackmail", to Theo Hartnell in his study. To my astonishment, the boy returned a minute later and, with a distinctly peevish expression, advised us that we were to follow him.

The hallway was decorated in the anonymous good taste of so many houses in that area, but the study of our host was a complete surprise. It was quite clear, as Katie had informed us, that no-one but Hartnell was allowed access to his room, for it was untidy to a quite dramatic degree. I observed his cot bed in the far corner of the room, and attempted to draw Holmes' attention to it, but if he heard my mutterings, he did not acknowledge them. The truly extraordinary feature of Theodore Hartnell's study must surely have been his collection of jewels. They were everywhere, on every surface, several atop books on the shelves. And they were all, without exception, a peculiar and distinctive shade of green. One particularly fine example, a necklace made up of these green beads, rested upon a small plinth on the dusty desk. Behind that desk, all but quivering with fear, sat Theodore Hartnell. He was a thin man, some forty years of age, I estimated, and his entire appearance described the pressure that had lately been brought to bear upon him. His tie was violently askew, his hair and moustache ill-groomed. His small, dark brown eyes were lost in large, sunken sockets. Their constant darting movements during our interview gave the distinct impression of a man on the brink of either madness or nervous exhaustion.

'What is the meaning of this?' he asked, querulously, throwing the card down upon the desk.

'If you are familiar with my name, Mr Hartnell,' Holmes replied, evenly, 'then you know that it is my business to be aware of that which others are not.'

'And what is it that you think you know about me?'

'That you are presently being blackmailed by a man named Reuben Fenster, a man who forced his way into your home two months ago and who has turned your life into a waking nightmare ever since.'

A look of puzzlement crossed Hartnell's face. 'What the devil? What ineffable twaddle!' he cried. 'Reuben Fenster, sir, is my lodger. He has lived under this roof for the last three years. Your suggestion that he is involved in anything illegal is nothing short of libellous!'

'Then why does Mr Fenster occupy your bedroom while you sleep in your study?' I indicated the cot. 'Do you deny it?'

'I loathe spies, sir, loathe them. You are, I suppose, Dr Watson? Well, doctor, my reasons for sleeping in my study are medical in nature but they are *my own*.'

'I supposed you might be fearful of intruders,' Holmes remarked, casually.

'Intruders?'

'Forgive me, burglars, I should say.'

'Then why say intruders?'

'Burglars intrude, do they not? I should have thought that a gentleman with so fine a collection…' With uncharacteristic effrontery, Holmes reached for the necklace on the plinth, only to have his hand slapped away by Hartnell as though he were disciplining a naughty schoolboy.

'Mr Sherlock Holmes,' he said, coldly. 'You have burst into my home unannounced and unwelcome; you have proceeded to spew lies concerning my friends and have generally behaved in a most ungentlemanly fashion. I will not tolerate this foolishness one minute longer. I must ask you both to leave immediately.'

I followed Holmes' lead as he rose from his chair. 'If you decide to show sense in the days to come, Mr Hartnell, I may be contacted at the address on my card. May I wish you in the meantime an agreeable Christmas.'

Hartnell snatched up the card and tore it into tiny pieces before us. Then, rising from his chair, he darted for the door and threw it open.

'Get out!' he screamed. 'Both of you, out!'

I for one was only too happy to leave our infuriated host's presence at that moment, for he slammed the study door shut behind us with considerable force.

The intolerably smug page, Blatcher, opened the front door for us to depart, but we found our way blocked by a gentleman standing on the front step. He looked from one to the other of us in bemusement, before giving us a kindly smile. He stepped into the house and removed his stovepipe hat, revealing a shock of curly white hair.

'Mr Reuben Fenster I presume?' asked Holmes.

'My name, sir,' he replied in a soft voice. 'I apologise if we have met in the past, I am afraid I do not recall…'

'My name is Sherlock Holmes, and this is my colleague, Dr Watson.'

Fenster nodded. 'The season's greetings to you both, gentlemen. Oh! Ah! Sherlock Holmes, did you say?'

'That is correct, Mr Fenster.'

'Is something amiss?'

'What do you imagine might be amiss, sir?' I asked impertinently.

'I really cannot imagine. Are you, perhaps, friends of Mr Hartnell?'

'Acquaintances,' Holmes replied. 'We were paying a call upon him to wish him a merry Christmas.'

'How charming! I suppose that when one hears the name of Sherlock Holmes, one always expects that some fearful villainy must be afoot. It must be very tiresome for you. I am very sorry to see that you are leaving, gentlemen, for I should have enjoyed hearing some of your stories, they must be fascinating. I am afraid my own life is very dull by comparison.'

'Well, I have no doubt we shall meet again very soon. Good evening, Mr Fenster.'

Delicate snowflakes were beginning to fall as we stepped out onto the street. Rather than take a cab straight away, Holmes suggested that the chill air might aid our thought processes.

'I wish to introspect, for there is much in this case that is not clear to me. Indeed, I may say that our little excursion has furnished us with several new questions, but few answers. Tell me, Watson, what was your impression of Reuben Fenster?'

'Too good to be true, I thought. The kindly nature, the soft voice, all undoubtedly part of an elaborate act.'

'I found him very interesting, particularly his right shirt-cuff. And what of Theodore Hartnell?'

'Fenster clearly has him terrified out of his wits. I am certain that not one word of truth crossed his lips during the entire interview. I only wish that Katie could have been there to confront him with her testimony.'

'Yes, that would indeed have been most enlightening. His collection is quite a prideful thing.'

'Emeralds, are they not?'

'Jade, Watson, and a particularly rare sort of jade – Fei Tsui, which is valuable in itself rather than for the way it is cut. The necklace is surely the pride of his collection; fifty-one beads, about six carats each, I should say.'

'I did wonder why a bachelor should keep an item of woman's jewellery on display. I'm afraid I know as little about jade as I do about Chinese pottery.'

'We must correct that deficiency one day, Watson. In the meantime, you will be pleased to hear that I also am of the opinion that we have been lied to. The difficulty now is in determining which lies are significant and which are mere confabulations. In your opinion, doctor, does Hartnell indeed suffer from a severe back complaint?'

I felt somewhat uncomfortable being asked to provide a medical opinion without the benefit of an examination, but I knew that Holmes respected my judgement as well as my caution in such matters. 'I should say,' I responded, after taking a moment to compose my thoughts, 'that there is nothing unusual about the curvature of the spine. From his actions when he became excitable, I should also say that his movement is in no way impeded by physical pain. Of course, I am not a specialist.'

'But I *am*, Watson – a specialist in crime. And I think it highly unlikely that too much time will pass before my speciality becomes an urgent matter in this case. I sense that there is a malevolent force at work here, but I regret that I am unable at present to identify its true nature. I pray that the moment of clarity may not come too late…'

I was weary after our long walk and upon our return to Baker Street I was only too eager to retire to bed. Holmes, however, announced that he was planning another all night sitting during which he would usually consider a problem from all conceivable angles until he was satisfied that he had hit upon the solution. In this instance, however, I was quite perplexed by this approach; here I had heard what he had heard, I had seen what he had seen, and yet it still appeared to me that we were faced with a straightforward case of blackmail. Why had our excursion unsettled Holmes so? I knew that it would be useless to question him upon this subject until he felt fully confident that he was in possession of all the facts and had arranged them in a coherent order.

Thus I left him, coiled up in his favourite armchair, consuming ounce after poisonous ounce of his favourite brand of coarse tobacco as he studied the snowflakes falling past our window at an ever-increasing rate.

It was not yet light when I was awakened from my slumber by a tugging at my shoulder. I opened my eyes blearily to discover Sherlock Holmes, still dressed in his clothes of the previous evening, at the side of my bed. 'We must return to Lancaster Gate at once,' he said. 'Shirt-cuffs.'

It was no easy task to find a cab at such an hour during the festive season, but the fates were with us, and we were soon speeding through the snow-filled streets on our way back to the residence of Mr Theodore Hartnell. Holmes said little during the journey, save that his every instinct cried out against him leaving the case in its present condition.

His worst fears were confirmed when we arrived at the

house we had left a few hours before. The sunlight was just striking the rooftops, but a small crowd of ghoulish onlookers had already begun to form.

'As I feared Watson,' Holmes murmured as we began to force our way through the crowds. The smartly-dressed police inspector, who stood solemnly in the doorway, had no difficulty in identifying us. Despite the passing years, nor did we in recognising him.

'Mr Holmes and Dr Watson!' gasped Inspector Lanner. 'Long time. The Abernetty case in '85, wasn't it? I had no idea you were mixed up in this. It's a bad business.'

'There has been murder done, then?' I asked.

'That's right, doctor. Mr Reuben Fenster was strangled in his bed some time during the night.'

'A passer-by, on his way back from some seasonal jollification saw the front door open,' Lanner explained. 'The alarm was quickly raised and this Fenster was discovered dead in his bed. No weapons used, just the killer's bare hands. Whoever he was, he was obviously admitted by a confederate inside the house, for there has been no damage done to the door. The page, whose name I understand is Blatcher, cannot be found. The maid and the cook have been searching for him.'

A thought struck me. 'Holmes, the bundled-up man in the street! Might he not have been another of Fenster's victims?'

'Victims, doctor?' said Lanner. 'Forgive me, I know nothing about any victims.'

'We have reason to believe, Inspector,' I explained, 'that Reuben Fenster was a master blackmailer, that he held the owner of this house, Mr Theodore Hartnell, in a grip of terror.'

'Oh, so he owns this place, does he? Odd sort of fellow. It took us ages to get him to come round properly, and a right state he's been in ever since. Practically tearing his hair out.'

'Mr Holmes and I were advised by Mr Hartnell's maid, Katie, that she had seen the page talking to a mysterious man outside the house. It would seem that the young imp, in addition to taking orders from Fenster, must have accepted payment to admit his killer during the night.'

Lanner clapped his hands together. 'So it all comes down to finding the man, eh, Mr Holmes?'

Holmes, who had not participated in this exchange at all, appeared no longer to be even listening. He was instead, crouched on the floor in the hallway, examining a small, dark stain on the carpeting.

'It is blood, Watson,' he proclaimed.

I crouched down also and put my finger to the sticky patch. 'Undoubtedly it is blood,' I agreed. 'But Reuben Fenster was strangled to death.'

'Might not the blood belong to the murderer?' Lanner suggested.

'Are there any stains in the bedroom, where the killing occurred?' Holmes asked. The inspector shook his head. 'Or a weapon? It is inconceivable that the killer should have taken it away with him.'

'It is possible that the bloodstain has nothing to do with the matter, then.'

'You are no Athelney Jones, Lanner. You do not seriously believe that. Besides that, I can promise you that that mark was not there when I examined the hall earlier.'

Holmes and Lanner proceeded upstairs to search Fenster's room for evidence of his criminal activities. There was little that I could do to assist, Fenster's body having been removed prior to our arrival. In any case, I was more concerned for our young client and her master. I found them both in his study. Katie, clad in a thick grey dressing gown, was attempting to console Hartnell, as he sobbed like a baby. Like Holmes, he was still dressed in his clothes of the day before, but he appeared even wilder than on our last meeting.

'Compose yourself, Mr Hartnell,' I said in a firm voice. 'This behaviour is hardly seemly.'

'Go to the devil, sir!' he cried, raising his head. His eyes were blurred with tears, and his pupils had contracted markedly.

'Mr Hartnell, sir, you must listen to Dr Watson,' Katie urged him. 'He and Mr Holmes have lots of experience of dealing with criminals. Whatever has gone on here, they will get to the bottom of it, of that you can be sure.'

This speech did little to raise his spirits, and his reply became inaudible as he began to whimper. This led to further tears and it became obvious that neither of us could say anything to break him out of it. I signalled for Katie to join me at a discreet distance from her distressed employer.

'Katie,' I whispered, 'I am not easy in my mind about you remaining on the premises after what has happened.'

'I appreciate your concern, doctor, I really do, but surely the danger has passed, hasn't it? Mr Fenster must have been killed by someone else he was blackmailing, mustn't he?'

'If that is so, then why is Hartnell so upset?' I asked. 'Indeed, he seems more so since Fenster's death. I am convinced that he has not told us all and he is still at risk from some threat.'

Katie appeared resolute. 'If that is so, doctor,' she said, levelly, 'then I must stay at his side. I came to you for help because I feared Mr Hartnell was in danger. If he is still in danger, I cannot leave him now.'

I gave her a pat on the shoulder. 'You are a brave girl, Katie. I urge you to contact us if there are any developments.'

Still feeling ill at ease, I left them as Holmes and Lanner were descending the stairs.

171

'There is little more to be learned here,' Holmes sighed. 'We may both return to Baker Street and catch up on our sleep.'

'I am bound to say that I agree with Mr Holmes' explanation of a private feud between the late Mr Fenster and this mysterious bundled-up man,' Lanner added. When we track down the boy Blatcher, he will undoubtedly tell us what we need to know. But the occupants of this house have had a most unsettled night. I think it only right that Scotland Yard should leave them in peace.'

Having been denied any further sensation following the removal of Reuben Fenster's corpse, the crowd had dispersed by the time we stepped out onto the street. Their recent presence was obvious even to a non-detective; the shoes of a dozen onlookers had transformed the snow, once a virginal white, into a vile grey slush.

Luck was with us once again, and I was able to summon a cab almost immediately. I noticed as it ground to a halt before us, the ruts of several other cab wheels – undoubtedly the one that had deposited us there some hours earlier, and the one in which Inspector Lanner had arrived. Holmes insisted that we wait for the policeman, who was presently taking his leave of the inconsolable Hartnell, before setting off for home.

'Did you find any trace of Fenster's blackmail papers?' I asked. Holmes shook his head in reply. 'It is highly probable that the killer took them with him. As the inspector says, he was most likely one of Fenster's victims, after all.'

I apprised Holmes of the details of my failed attempt to persuade Hartnell to confide in us.

'His enemy is dead and yet he whimpers as though... No doubt I am being very dense, but I can make nothing of it.'

'Do you know your la Rouchefoucauld, Watson? "There are no fools so troublesome as those who have some wit".

It saddens me to say it, but it appears that I am the fool in question.'

Lanner appeared at that moment, rubbing his arms vigorously. His coat, although in the height of fashion, was a poor defence against the cruel winter weather.

'These are the crucial hours, Lanner,' Holmes told him. 'You must follow my instructions to the letter if we are to prevent a third murder.'

'A Third? You mean a second.'

'Oh, yes; no doubt that is what I must have meant,' said Holmes, enigmatically.

It was not until I had enjoyed another brief sleep and a satisfying breakfast, courtesy of Mrs Hudson, that I realized that the date was now the 24th of December, Christmas Eve. I recollected that the day before, I had expected this Christmas to be a grim affair. With the sudden death of Reuben Fenster, scoundrel though he undoubtedly was, that expectation had become a certainty. Holmes, to my surprise, had made no mention of our early morning adventure, nor had he given any indication that he intended to leave Baker Street at all that day. Instead, he spent what little remained of the morning enjoying his cherrywood pipe and updating his index.

A crash downstairs caused me to jump to my feet.

'What on earth was that?' I said.

'I prefer never to guess if at all possible, but I should imagine that it was the sound of Mrs Hudson dropping our breakfast things, having observed an upsetting spectacle from the window. And now she is again taking the stairs at a considerable pace. This talent for short uphill sprints is a revelation to me, Watson. I never get that woman's limits.'

The door to our room burst open to reveal our startled landlady, a fork hanging uselessly from her fingers.

'Mr Holmes! That nicely-dressed policeman Mr Lanner has just arrived, and young Katie is with him. Mr Holmes

– she's wearing handcuffs!'

'A wise precaution, I think. Mrs Hudson, I regret to say that a callous and utterly ruthless criminal has exploited your good nature. If you would be so good as to stay, I will explain how we were all deceived by this devious young woman. Watson, I fancy that I hear Lanner's ring at the door. Would you be so good as to save Mrs Hudson the trouble of answering it?'

'This case will make a stir, gentlemen, you mark my words.' Lanner announced, excitedly. 'Why, I should not be surprised if several of London's greatest financial institutions do not fall as a result of Sir Norris's arrest.'

'Sir Norris?' I asked, bewildered.

'Sir Norris Whitehead,' Katie replied, in a manner and accent I had not heard before. 'My father.'

She was dressed now in the height of quiet good taste, with matching gloves and shoes, and a short-brimmed hat tilted at a fashionably rakish angle. Save for those sparkling green eyes, I barely recognised her as the woman who pleaded for our assistance in the same room a day earlier.

'We nabbed three of them at the Capital and Counties Bank.' The inspector continued. 'This young lady eluded us for a time, but I soon caught up with her. You will never guess, Mr Holmes, the cabman was Sir Norris' son! It seems they paid some fellow for the use of his growler for the night. They are all down at the Yard, but I thought that you would like to see "Miss Whitehall" once more, considering the amount of trouble she has caused. I also thought you would enjoy reading these.'

He extracted a bundle of papers from his pocket and handed them to Holmes, who studied them with evident satisfaction. Katie eyed him contemptuously.

'Well, sir, are they what you expected?' Lanner asked.

'They are more than satisfactory,' Holmes replied.

'Watson, may I introduce Miss Katherine Whitehead, daughter of the noted industrialist Sir Norris Whitehead and without doubt the most calculating villainess to have tested my wits in many a year. You will forgive me, I am sure, if I smoke, Miss Whitehead. If everyone would take a seat, I believe that both Watson and Mrs Hudson are still owed an explanation.'

'I must admit that there is still much about this case that is not clear to me,' added the inspector.

'You *do* surprise me,' his prisoner muttered.

'We'll have no more of that, miss.'

'I explained to Lanner as much of the matter as was obvious at that time when we were supposedly searching Fenster's room for evidence of his activities as a blackmailer. You were extremely clever, Miss Whitehead, in persuading us to distrust everyone's word but your own. Fenster was a villain and could not be believed, Blatcher was under his spell and would lie for his new master, Hartnell was in fear of his lodger and would be too terrified to speak the truth. Most cunning. But I began to experience some doubts when we encountered Fenster unexpectedly on Hartnell's doorstep.'

'You mentioned something about his right shirt-cuff,' I reminded him.

'Quite correct, Watson. To the trained observer, the inveterate letter-writer leaves seven separate indications of that fact upon his person, ink-stains on his shirt-cuffs being the most obvious. I noticed when he removed his stovepipe hat that Fenster was right handed, but I did not see any ink-stains on his cuff, nor were there any of the six other indicators. Miss Whitehead's claim that Fenster spent all his days writing letters, apparently to his blackmail victims, was therefore a lie. By logical extrapolation, the assertion that Blatcher the page posted these non-existent letters was also a lie. If two elements of her tale could be dismissed as untruths, might not her entire story be a total fabrication? I said nothing at that time, though, for I was still troubled by her assertion that she had seen Blatcher deep in conversation with a suspicious character in the street. Now, all her other lies were concerned with the goings-on within the house, so what was the significance of this lie?'

'Kindly do not speak about me as though I were not here,' snapped the young woman I had known as Katie.

'Some hours later,' Holmes continued, ignoring her, 'it came to me. We were intended to believe that Fenster had an unseen enemy who might wish to gain entrance to the house and do him harm. That much of the scheme I had divined, but I arrived at Lancaster Gate too late to prevent his death by strangulation.'

'What, then, was so extraordinary about this lodger?' asked Lanner.

'Nothing whatsoever, inspector, save for his extreme ordinariness. It was for that reason that Hartnell selected him some three years ago, not two months as this lady assured us.'

'Selected him for what purpose, Holmes?' I asked. 'My head is in a whirl. What part was played in the crime by the page, and where is he at present? Why were we consulted by Katie- this young woman - and why did she wish to deceive us?'

'Those are all quite apposite questions, doctor. You have summed up my difficulties at that time succinctly and well, bravo. The answers to all of those questions were to be found in the bloodstain I discovered in the hallway following the murder. It was not Fenster's, for he was strangled, nor did it come from the intruder. Hartnell slept through the entire incident, drugged by Miss Whitehead, who brought him his evening meal as usual.'

'Drugged? Of course, I did notice something unusual about his pupils, but I put it down to his excessive weeping. The blood must surely have belonged to the

176

page.'

'Struck down from behind by a heavy object wielded by our client.'

'You wicked girl!' snapped Mrs Hudson, who had remained silent thus far.

'I imagine that Blatcher's body can now be found floating in the Thames, if it has not completely frozen over. Her father removed the corpse and placed it in the waiting Hansom before murdering Fenster in his bed. I noticed that you were examining the wheel-ruts outside the house, Watson. No doubt you saw that they belonged to three different vehicles: our own cab, the inspector's, and Whitehead's. It was planned that it should appear as though Blatcher had allowed the intruder into the house and had subsequently fled. We were to corroborate Katie's version of events when approached by Scotland Yard. It seems that I am a prophet without honour in his own land.'

'But the story could not stand up to scrutiny,' I pointed out.

'Nor did it need to. She required only a few more hours under Hartnell's roof now that he believed his life in danger and the mythical Katie Whitehall a loyal and trustworthy servant.'

'But why?' three voices asked in unison.

'Is it not yet clear to you that it was Hartnell, not Fenster, who was the blackmailer of Lancaster Gate?

'Hartnell had only one victim, Sir Norris Whitehead - a powerful and dangerous man. He was in possession of papers which proved that in former times, Norris Whitehead – as he then was – had links to the criminal organisation controlled by Professor Moriarty. Whitehead severed his ties to Moriarty long before the arrest of the gang in '91, but he could not be completely safe so long as Hartnell had these letters.' He held up the sheaf of papers handed to him by Inspector Lanner. 'Hartnell took care to cover his tracks-'

'The money was paid into the account of a "Mr A
Smithee" at the Capital and Counties Bank,' the policeman
interjected.
'But it was inevitable that his true identity should be
ascertained and his address discovered. What then? Sir
Norris might break in one night and kill Hartnell, but what
if he was unable to locate the papers before the police
arrived? Was the creation of Katie Whitehall your idea,
Miss?'
'The entire plot was mine, Mr Holmes.' She appeared
disconcertingly proud of the fact. 'It seemed simple
enough at first to enter Hartnell's employ and ascertain
where the letters might be hidden - obviously somewhere
in the study.'
'Yes, but where? No-one was allowed to enter that room,
and Hartnell hardly ever left it. He even slept there. The
closest you ever came to the study was to deliver his
meals.'
'Were you not taking a risk in giving us that information?'
I asked. Katie - Katherine Whitehead - refused to respond.
'Hardly, Watson. The fact would have been clear as soon
as we saw the state of the room. The use you made of
Fenster's presence, young lady, was most ingenious, if
utterly callous.'
'Thank-you.'
'Will somebody please explain Fenster's part in all this?' I
pleaded.
'Certainly, Watson. It was an act of almost equal
callousness on Hartnell's part to install a lodger in his
home who should appear to any outsider to be the master
of the house. Should anything happen to Fenster, Hartnell
would then have sufficient time to gather up his papers,
which I imagine were to be found inside the plinth on
which the jade necklace rested, and fly for his life. Miss
Whitehead simply decided to call his bluff. The plan could
not have succeeded were it not for Hartnell's mentally

fraught state. You played upon that nicely, madam, subtly taunting him about my dealings with criminals. After our departure, she ingratiated herself with her employer sufficiently to learn his immediate plans, which were to flee with the papers, having first withdrawn as much money as possible from the Smithee account. Once he had gone, she informed her father and brother where they might catch up with him.'

'Unfortunately for you, madam,' said the inspector, 'Mr Holmes had instructed me to follow Hartnell from a distance, and I caught up with all three of them!'

'If it is not too much trouble,' sighed the villainess, 'I believe I would like to join my family at Scotland Yard. A police cell would be preferable to this relentless cock-a-doodle-dooing.'

It seemed to me extraordinary that only a day had passed since our investigation had begun. Even after Lanner had left with his charge, I could still scarcely take it all in.

'I have met Sir Norris! We sat next to one another at Wimbledon! Why did I not see the family resemblance? Those green eyes!'

'Yes, they are quite distinctive, are they not? Do not chide yourself, Watson. We were both quite neatly deceived. I should have seen the truth sooner. There was a peculiarly subtle and cruel method behind the crime. Feline rather than canine.'

'A female Moriarty!' I shuddered at the thought.

'Cold, Watson? The fire is a bit low, I suppose. Incidentally, I owe you an apology. Until now, I have had neither the time nor the inclination to purchase you a Christmas present from Gamages. But in the past twenty-four hours, I have had occasion to alter my views on several subjects.'

'How so, Holmes?' I asked, settling myself into the chair nearest the fire.

'All Katie had to do was to strike Blatcher with a blunt instrument. Had that drop of blood not fallen I might never have solved the case and three murderers would have been free to kill again. A single drop of blood falls against all logic, all sense! There was no reason in the world for it to do so. I confess I had begun to lose faith in the notion of some guiding force behind our universe other than mere chance. I no longer have any such doubts. It is, after all, the time for miracles. I now feel justified, my dear Watson, in offering you the compliments of the season.'

ABOUT THE AUTHOR

Matthew J Elliott is a writer and dramatist whose articles, fiction and reviews have appeared in the magazines *SHERLOCK*, *Sherlock Holmes Mystery Magazine*, *Total DVD* and *Scarlet Street*.

For the radio, he has scripted episodes of *The Further Adventures of Sherlock Holmes*, *The Classic Adventures of Sherlock Holmes*, *Jeeves and Wooster*, *Wrath of the Titans*, *Logan's Run: Aftermath*, *Fangoria's Dreadtime Stories*, *Raffles the Gentleman Thief*, *The Twilight Zone*, *The Father Brown Mysteries*, *Kincaid the Strangeseeker*, *The Adventures of Harry Nile*, *The Thinking Machine*, *The Perry Mason Radio Dramas*, *Vincent Price Presents*, *Fantom House of Horrors*, *Allan Quatermain*, *The Prince and the Pauper* and the Audie Award-nominated *New Adventures of Mickey Spillane's Mike Hammer*. He is the creator of *The Hilary Caine Mysteries*, which first aired in 2005.

His stage play *An Evening With Jeeves and Wooster* was performed at the Palace Theatre, Grapevine, Texas in 2007.

He is the author of *Sherlock Holmes on the Air*, published by MX in 2012, and he has contributed to the Sherlockian short story volumes *The Game's Afoot*, *Curious Incidents 2* and *Gaslight Grimoire*. His Sherlock Holmes story *Art in the Blood* appeared in *The Mammoth Book of Best British Crime 8* in the UK, and *The Mammoth Book of Best British Crime 8* in the US. He is the editor of the collections *The Whisperer in Darkness*, *The Horror in the Museum*, *The Haunter of the Dark* and *The Lurking Fear* by H P Lovecraft, *The Right Hand of Doom* and *The Haunter of the Ring* by Robert E Howard, and *A Charlie*

Chan Omnibus by Earl Derr Biggers.

Matthew is probably best-known as a writer/performer on RiffTrax.com, the online comedy experience from the makers of cult sci-fi TV series *Mystery Science Theater 3000* (*MST3K* to the initiated).

He also writes comic books for Bluewater.
Matthew does nothing in his spare time, because he never seems to have any.

He lives in the North-West of England with his wife and daughter.

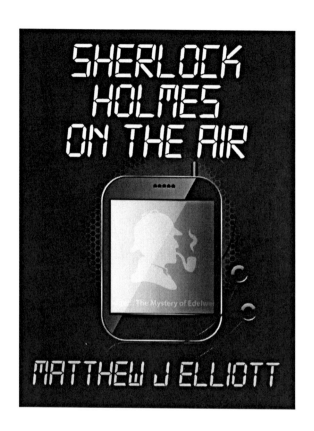

"*M J Elliott contributed his first script in 2003 and is now one of the most prolific and intelligent writers in the field. If you ve ever listened to a radio play and asked yourself, How did they do that? or even, Why did they do that? you ll love Sherlock Holmes on the Air*"

Sherlock Holmes Society of London

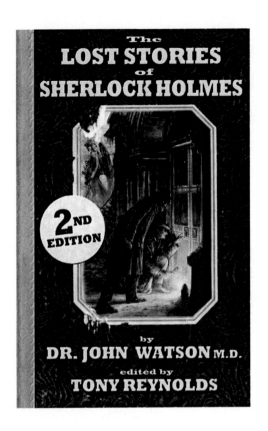

"*The most pleasing aspect is the way that the book is presented in the style of the original Strand Magazine. The typeface is the same (or very close to) and the illustrations are excellent. In fact they almost make you feel like Sidney Paget had been resurrected to produce them. All in all this is very much one of the better collections of pastiche stories. For me personally I very much like the fact that the author has stuck to the spirit of the originals.*"

Alistair Duncan

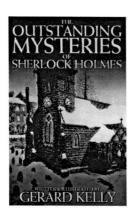

Also from MX Publishing, two more short story collections:

The Outstanding Mysteries of Sherlock Holmes

The Untold Adventures of Sherlock Holmes

and many more novels, novellas, ebooks, travel guides, and biographies.

www.mxpublishing.com

www.mxpublishing.co.uk

Lightning Source UK Ltd.
Milton Keynes UK
UKOW05f0135030813

214791UK00001B/20/P